FROM APPLAUSE TO INSULTS

"You probably know some of the other stars in my movie," Taffy went on. "Raven Blaine . . . Paige Kramer. We got to be super friends."

"So I suppose all your Hollywood friends are better than your friends back here in good old boring Wacko!" challenged Tammy Lucero.

"Right," said Marcie Bee. "I'm surprised you'd even sit with Shawnie now that you have big-deal movie stars for friends."

Taffy looked at them in horror. She opened her mouth to reply, but Shelly Bramlett cut her off.

"Oh, I just *love* my new friends," Shelly said in a falsetto voice, which Taffy knew was supposed to be an imitation of her own voice. "They're all *sooooo* famous!"

Laughter broke out around the room.

"Hey, guys. Wait a minute," Shawnie yelled over the noise, but no one was paying any attention to her. Then turning to Taffy, she said, "Come on. Let's get out of here."

Taffy couldn't speak because of the tears gathering behind her eyes. *What was wrong with everybody? Why didn't they understand?*

NOBODY LIKES TAFFY SINCLAIR

Betsy Haynes

A BANTAM SKYLARK BOOK®
NEW YORK · TORONTO · LONDON · SYDNEY · AUCKLAND

RL 5, 009–012

NOBODY LIKES TAFFY SINCLAIR
A Bantam Skylark Book / July 1991

*Skylark Books is a registered trademark of Bantam Books,
a division of Bantam Doubleday Dell Publishing Group, Inc.
Registered in U.S. Patent and Trademark Office and elsewhere.*

ISBN 0-553-15877-5

Published simultaneously in the United States and Canada

Bantam Books are published by Bantam Books, a division of Bantam Doubleday Dell Publishing Group, Inc. Its trademark, consisting of the words "Bantam Books" and the portrayal of a rooster, is Registered in U.S. Patent and Trademark Office and in other countries. Marca Registrada. Bantam Books, 666 Fifth Avenue, New York, New York 10103.

PRINTED IN THE UNITED STATES OF AMERICA
CWO   0 9 8 7 6 5 4 3 2 1

1 ✸

𝒯affy Sinclair stared out the windshield as her mother turned the car into the long driveway leading to the front of Wakeman Junior High. It had been six long weeks since she had left home and gone to Hollywood to star in an after-school movie. Taffy had auditioned for the leading role in *Nobody Likes Tiffany Stafford* and won out over one hundred and fifty other girls. It would be shown on national television in a few weeks. Last night she and her mother had taken the long flight back from Los Angeles International Airport to La Guardia Airport in New York City. The plane had not landed until almost midnight, and the rest of the ride home in the car was just a sleepy blur.

Everything looks the same, she thought. Yellow buses lined one side of the drive, and kids milled about on the broad lawn and congregated near the doors.

"Look, Mother! There's Mona Vaughn. Oh, there's Shane Arrington, too," she said happily.

"Of course, dear," said her mother with a touch of impatience in her voice. "Now, don't forget to take all your books and to turn in the lessons that you did with your tutor on the movie set to each of your teachers."

Taffy sighed. "I won't forget. I'll do it as soon as I get to class."

How could I forget? she thought, feeling suddenly unsure about going back to being an ordinary seventh-grader after living the glamorous life of an actress. She wondered for the millionth time how everyone at Wakeman would treat her, now that she was a movie star. Would she fit in again, or feel terribly out of place? At least I have Shawnie Pendergast, she thought, remembering how anxious her best friend had been for her to come home. I can't wait to see her and tell her all about Hollywood.

And then there was Cory Dillon. Cory was an eighth-grader who had moved to town from Louisiana last year. He had a soft southern accent and a gorgeous smile, and practically every girl in school had had a crush on him since he started Wakeman's first rock band, The Dreadful Alternatives. He had asked her out a month before she went to Hollywood, and they had dated every single weekend before she left. She had been sure then that it was just a matter of time before he asked her to go steady, and they had written a few times while she was away. Still, six weeks was a long time, and she couldn't help wondering if he still liked her.

Taffy took a deep breath to calm her jitters and got out of the car. She loaded the books into her arms and headed for the front door. An instant later she stopped, staring at Dekeisha Adams, who was coming up the front sidewalk in bright pink, fuzzy bedroom slippers. Taffy did a double take as her eyes traveled up the tall black girl from the bedroom slippers to the knee-length pink sleep shirt sticking out below her jacket.

"Dekeisha?" Taffy whispered in astonishment. "What on earth are you wearing?"

Dekeisha caught sight of Taffy just then and hurried toward her. "Hey, Taffy! Is that really you? Welcome back from Hollywood! When did you get home?"

"Last night," said Taffy, feeling relieved that the first person to greet her was so friendly. She squinted at Dekeisha's clothes again and asked, "But why are you dressed that way? Are you in a play or something?"

Dekeisha twirled around to show off her outfit. "It's Pajama Day," she said, grinning. "But I guess you wouldn't know about Pajama Day, since we just voted on it last week. Every month we're going to have one day where everybody comes to school in costume if they want to. This month it's Pajama Day. Next month it's going to be Clash Day. You know, nothing you wear can match. Then we're going to have School Colors Day, stuff like that. It's just for fun, and it ought to be a blast."

"Gosh, I wish I'd known," said Taffy, frowning. "I'll probably be the only one at school wearing regular clothes." *And not fitting in*, she added silently. *Just like I thought*.

"Hey, maybe we'll have Movie Star Day, and everybody can come as a famous movie star. Then I'll put on a blond wig and come as Taffy Sinclair." Dekeisha laughed good-naturedly over her shoulder and headed into the building.

Taffy went in too, noticing immediately that lots of girls were wearing bedroom slippers. Some of the slippers were the floppy kind with open backs, but the most popular were the huge fuzzy ones that looked like animal heads. Almost all of the girls were wearing pajama-type outfits, but she noticed that most of the boys seemed to be wearing their regular clothes. Still, she felt terribly out of place as she made her way through the halls to her locker.

"Look! There she is. The movie star!"

Taffy felt a rush of excitement. She dropped the combination lock she had been working on and spun around to face the three eighth-grade girls who had stopped nearby. All three of them were dressed for

bed. Taffy remembered seeing them around school before. She wasn't sure of their names, but she was glad
that they had recognized her.

"Did you really go to Hollywood?" asked one of the
girls, who Taffy thought was named Josie something-
or-other. She had brown hair that hung straight to her
shoulders and wore a flannel granny gown and matching nightcap.

"Oh, yes," Taffy assured her. "I had the starring role
in an after-school movie called *Nobody Likes Tiffany
Stafford*. And I got to meet lots of famous movie stars,
and I had my own chauffeur and limousine, and . . ."

The tall blonde standing next to Josie nudged her
and whispered something.

Taffy blinked. Had she said something wrong? "But
I still had to go to school. I had my own private tutor."
She paused again, feeling suddenly panicky. "Is there
something special you'd like to know about?" she
asked.

The girls exchanged glances. "No," said Josie. "Not
really." The three of them stared at her for a moment,
then moved on down the hall, leaving Taffy looking
after them in puzzlement.

"Why were they so rude?" she mumbled to herself.
"I mean, they asked me if I went to Hollywood, didn't
they?"

She turned back to her locker and began working
the combination again. "Fumble fingers," she whis-

pered in frustration as the lock failed to open. She
spun it and began the combination again. It was left
seven—right fifteen—left nine, wasn't it? she thought.
Surely she hadn't forgotten it in just six weeks.

"Left seven," she murmured, "right fif . . ."

"Oh, Taffy! There you are!"

Taffy recognized the voice this time. It was Shawnie
Pendergast, her best friend. Shawnie was walking up
the hall toward her with Kimm Taylor, who was the
singer for The Dreadful Alternatives.

Taffy couldn't help chuckling. Shawnie had on a pajama sweatsuit with a teddy bear on the front and carried a matching bear under one arm.

"I'm so glad you're back!" Shawnie cried, racing up
to Taffy and giving her a big hug. "It seems like six
months since you left instead of six weeks."

"Oh, hi, Shawnie. Believe me, I'm glad to see you,
too," Taffy assured her, and she meant it. After years
of rivalry with Jana Morgan and her friends in The
Fabulous Five with no one but homely Mona Vaughn
to take her side, Taffy had discovered Shawnie Pendergast, and they had hit it off immediately. They both
loved clothes and had long blond hair, although
Shawnie also had a sprinkling of cinnamon freckles on
her nose.

Smiling at Shawnie, Taffy said, "I've got so much to
tell you that I don't know where to begin." Then, rolling her eyes, she added, "There are some things that
can't be put into letters, if you know what I mean."

"You bet I do," said Shawnie, laughing, "and I can't wait to hear *everything*. Kimm and I have been talking about how exciting it must have been out there. You know Kimm, don't you, Taffy?"

Taffy blinked at Kimm. She was wearing a beautiful red silk kimono, which looked especially nice with her long, straight black hair and almond eyes. Of course she knew Kimm, but there was something in the way Shawnie said it that gave her a funny feeling.

"Hi, Kimm," she said.

"Listen, I've got to run," said Kimm. "I need to get a book from the media center before the bell rings."

"See you later," Shawnie called out as Kimm raced down the hall. Then, turning to Taffy, she said, "Kimm's awfully nice. Did you know that her grand-mother was born in China?"

"No," answered Taffy, feeling a stab of jealousy. Shawnie was supposed to be *her* best friend. So why was she talking so much about Kimm?

"Cory and I just got your postcards yesterday saying you'd be back today," said Shawnie. "Have you seen him yet?"

"No," replied Taffy, adding quickly. "I hope he still likes me. Six weeks is a long time to be gone."

"Don't worry. He still likes you—a lot! Now, come on," Shawnie urged her. "Hang up your jacket, and let's see if we can find him."

Taffy nodded and tried her combination again. This

time the lock popped open. She hung her jacket on a hook and carefully stacked her books on the top shelf, keeping out only the ones she would need for her morning classes.

"Have you noticed how everyone's staring at me? I know it's not because I don't have on my pajamas," she said a few minutes later as she and Shawnie strolled down the hallway. "I mean, it's true that I went to a lot of Hollywood parties and met tons of famous stars, but . . ."

"Yeah, like Raven Blaine," chimed in Shawnie, raising her eyebrows. "That had to be a totally *awesome* experience."

Taffy felt her face color slightly at the mention of the handsome boy whom she had met while she was in Hollywood. Raven Blaine was one of the biggest teen idols in the world, and she fondly touched the small gold star on the delicate chain that hung around her neck. Her name was engraved on one side, and it had been a gift from Raven to celebrate her movie debut.

Taffy sighed at the memory. In her wildest dreams she had never imagined that someone like Raven Blaine could possibly be interested in her, much less send her presents. She had wanted to pinch herself each time they were together to make sure it was true. But Raven was in Hollywood, and she was here. She wasn't sure how long it would take to get over her crush on him. But Cory Dillon was her boyfriend here at home, and she cared about him, too.

"You didn't tell Cory about Raven, did you?" she asked quickly.

"Of course not," said Shawnie, giving Taffy a reassuring smile. "And what he doesn't know won't hurt him, right?"

Taffy returned Shawnie's smile, but her friend's words had given her a sinking feeling. "I sure hope not," she murmured.

2*

As she walked along the hallway with Shawnie, Taffy could see heads turning her way and kids whispering as she went past. Obviously they were talking about her. The idea made her tingle all over. Probably everybody was dying to hear what it was like to be a movie star, and lots of kids were bound to be jealous.

It's *definitely* good to be back, she thought.

When they reached the stairway, Shawnie wiggled her fingers good-bye and headed upstairs to her homeroom. "I'll see you in the cafeteria at noon, okay?" she called back over her shoulder.

"Right," Taffy responded. She rushed toward her own homeroom, giggling to herself at seeing so many kids in their pajamas.

11

At the same time, she was still on the lookout for Cory. She could hardly wait to see him again. Taffy was checking for Cory among the faces in the crowd coming toward her when she heard voices behind her.

"Dekeisha Adams just told me that she saw Taffy Sinclair in front of school a few minutes ago," exclaimed Beth Barry. Beth was one of The Fabulous Five, the group of girls who had been Taffy's worst enemies at Mark Twain Elementary and had even had a club against her in fifth grade.

"Wow. I wonder if she has on a black satin negligee for Pajama Day," Katie Shannon remarked sarcastically.

"Probably," said Beth. "It would be just like her. Taffy must have just gotten home from Hollywood. Can you imagine how much more stuck-up she'll be, now that she's a movie star?"

Taffy stiffened and listened as the girls went on talking about her, obviously unaware that she was so near.

"You can say that again," said Jana Morgan. "It's a shame, too. She was starting to seem pretty nice just before she left."

"Big deal," sniffed Melanie Edwards. "Now she'll probably make up all kinds of stories about how she's been going out with guys like Ralph Macchio or Fred Savage or Raven Blaine. Some kids might actually believe her."

"Oh, come on," said Katie. "Nobody would believe *that*."

An instant later the four friends had turned down a corridor and disappeared out of earshot. Taffy ducked out of the crowd and leaned against the wall, her eyes wide with horror at what she had just heard.

But I DID go out with Raven Blaine! she wanted to shout. *And not only that, he wants to date me if I ever go back to Hollywood!*

But you don't dare tell them, warned a little voice in her mind. If you do, Cory might find out and not want to go out with you anymore. Then you'd really be out of luck, since Raven is so far away.

That doesn't leave me much choice, Taffy thought dejectedly. She pushed herself away from the wall and rejoined the crowd of students hurrying to class. I'll just have to keep quiet about Raven.

When she reached room 107, Taffy slid into her seat and glanced around to see if anyone was looking at her. Nobody was. Most of them were whispering together or watching the parade of pajama-clad girls enter the room. Most of the girls, including Jana Morgan, Laura McCall, and two of Laura's best friends, Tammy Lucero and Melissa McConnell, wore sweatsuit-type outfits or oversize T's with pictures on the front.

When Clarence Marshall walked in, Randy Kirwan and Shane Arrington winked at each other, and Shane called out, "Hey, Clarence. Where are your Bart Simpson jammies?" The whole room burst out laughing.

Mona Vaughn and Matt Zeboski came in next, holding hands. Neither of them was wearing pajamas.

Taffy sighed and watched a dozen or so others enter the room, none of them the least concerned with her presence.

Finally the bell rang, and Mr. Neal came in, wearing a long maroon bathrobe over his street clothes. A few giggles broke out as he went straight to his desk. "Good morning, class," he said as if there were nothing the least bit unusual going on. Then he looked toward Taffy and smiled. "Welcome back, Taffy. I got a note from Mr. Bell that you would be back with us today. How was Hollywood?"

Little ripples of excitement raced through Taffy. Now everyone was looking at her. "It was terrific. *Really* terrific," she assured him.

Suddenly Mona Vaughn jumped to her feet.

"Oh, Mr. Neal. Let Taffy tell us all about it," she begged. "It sounds so exciting."

Mr. Neal seemed to be considering the idea, and Taffy glanced sideways at Mona. Mona had followed her around like a little lost puppy when they were at Mark Twain Elementary. In fact, she had practically worshiped Taffy. Taffy had long ago decided that Mona was her biggest fan.

"All right, Mona," said Mr. Neal. "I think that's a good idea. Taffy, would you like to tell us a little bit about your experiences? I imagine that making a movie was very special."

Slowly Taffy rose to her feet. It was almost like being on the set again, seeing all those eyes trained on her, everyone waiting for her to speak. She cleared her throat and began talking. "Oh, yes. It was *very* special. It all began when I arrived at the Los Angeles airport, and Dollins, my very own chauffeur, was waiting to take me to my hotel in a long, black limousine."

Taffy paused as murmurs spread through the room. She tossed her long, blond hair over her shoulder and went on, "Everyone on the set was wonderful to me . . . the producer . . . the director . . . the other actors. Especially my costar, Raven Blaine."

The moment Raven's name was out of her mouth, Taffy regretted it. She hadn't meant to mention him to anyone but Shawnie.

Around the room several girls gasped at the mention of the handsome star.

"Oh, wow!" said Mona, melting down into her seat with a huge sigh. "Have my ears gone crazy, or did I just hear you say 'Raven Blaine'?"

"There's nothing wrong with your ears," Taffy said proudly, thinking that maybe it wouldn't hurt to talk about Raven as long as she was careful. "Not only was Raven my costar, but we also became *very* good friends."

Out of the corner of her eye Taffy saw Laura McCall stick a finger down her throat and pretend to gag. Her two friends put hands over their mouths to smother giggles.

Furious, Taffy looked straight at Laura and snapped, "It's the truth!"

"Oh, reeeeally?" asked Laura, her voice dripping with sarcasm.

"Really!" said Taffy, her eyes blazing with anger.

"Okay, ladies," Mr. Neal interjected. "That's enough. Besides, that's just about all the time we have today. Thanks, Taffy. Maybe you can tell us more tomorrow."

Taffy flashed Mr. Neal a big smile and sat down, ignoring Laura and her friends.

When the bell rang ending homeroom, Mr. Neal held up his hand for attention. "Thanks, all of you in pajamas, for not snoozing in class."

Taffy laughed along with everyone else and then scooped up her books and headed into the hall. She had taken only a few steps when she felt a tug on her arm and heard a voice say, "Wait up, Taffy. I've got to have your autograph."

It was Mona Vaughn, and she nearly dropped her books as she danced along beside Taffy and dug into her notebook for a sheet of paper at the same time.

"Here. Sign this," she said around the pencil sticking out of her mouth as she thrust the paper toward Taffy. "It'll be worth a fortune someday."

Taffy smiled and took the paper, glad that at least someone thought she was special. Shaking her head as Mona took the pencil out of her mouth and offered it to her, she said, "I have a pen right here."

Taffy couldn't help comparing this to the Saturday she had signed autographs in a Los Angeles mall while they were filming a shopping scene. It certainly was different. She sighed, then signed Mona's paper in big, swirling curlicues and handed it back to her with an appreciative smile.

Mona's eyes were glowing. "Thanks, Taffy. I'll treasure this forever. Honest. I really will."

If only everyone felt that way, Taffy thought wistfully as she watched Mona hurry on down the hall.

❂   ❂   ❂

Taffy was on her way to the cafeteria for lunch when she finally spotted Cory ahead of her in the crowded hall. He was walking with Craig Meacham, the drummer in The Dreadful Alternatives and the boy Shawnie had been dating while Taffy was in Hollywood. Taffy and Shawnie had promised each other that they would double-date the very first weekend that Taffy was back in town, but what if Cory didn't want to date her anymore?

The thought made her panic, and she walked faster, trying to push her way through the crowd and catch up with him. She darted between two eighth-grade girls in matching quilted bathrobes, murmured a quick apology for bumping them, and called out, "Cory! Wait up!"

Cory glanced back over his shoulder and stopped, causing the wave of kids moving in the same direction to veer around him. His face broke into a smile. "Taffy! I've been looking for you all morning."

Taffy couldn't remember when she'd felt so happy or so relieved. "I've been looking for you, too," she replied breathlessly. "Hey, don't you know that this is Pajama Day? Where are your pajamas?"

Craig Meacham got a sly grin on his face. "He's wearing them."

"Wearing them?" said Taffy. "He's wearing jeans."

Craig put a hand over his mouth, pretending to speak confidentially. "He sleeps in his underwear," he said loudly, and then broke up laughing.

Taffy felt her face turn tomato red. What a humiliating thing for Craig to say in public. She wondered if Cory was as embarrassed as she was. She was too afraid to look at him.

"See you two lovebirds around," called Craig. Still laughing, he disappeared into the crowd.

They moved slowly toward the cafeteria in uncomfortable silence for a moment until Cory finally cleared his throat a couple of times and said, "So I guess you got the filming finished okay?"

Taffy nodded. She took a deep breath while she got up the courage to look at Cory. To Taffy's relief he was smiling at her.

"Everything went super," she said, smiling back, thankful to get the conversation away from pajamas and underwear. "I'll tell you all about it when we have more time. It was just unbelievable. We even had a wrap-up party the last night at Raven Blaine's beach house in Malibu."

The mention of the handsome teen idol made her

heart stop for an instant. She could see the sweep of Raven's jet black hair across his forehead and the sparkle of his dark eyes as he looked at her, and her hand instinctively went to the star necklace she was wearing. But why had she mentioned his name again? Especially to Cory? She had already had one disaster today with Laura McCall and her friends. She didn't need another one. Besides, Raven Blaine is history, she told herself sternly, and Cory is *now*. She blinked away the memory of Raven and looked back at Cory.

"Raven Blaine has a beach house in Malibu? Wow! Maybe I should be jealous."

"Oh, no," Taffy assured him, the words almost sticking in her throat. "Don't be silly. Raven and I were just good friends."

Cory seemed satisfied, and her feeling of relief came back. Cory was the boy for her, and he was *here*. That was the only thing that mattered.

"You said you had been looking for me all morning," Taffy reminded him. "Anything special?"

Cory nodded. "It's about this weekend," he said. "Would you like to go to a movie Friday night? I know you just got home and everything, but . . ."

"I'd love to," Taffy said quickly.

"Great!" Cory grinned and looked relieved at the same time. "Well, I've got to go now. The guys are waiting. Talk to you later."

Taffy watched Cory bound toward the cafeteria. Life at Wakeman Junior High had just gotten one hundred percent better.

3

As Taffy stood in the hot-lunch line, she looked around for Shawnie. They had agreed to meet in the cafeteria at noon, and Taffy had hoped that Shawnie would get there first to hold a table. But she was nowhere in sight. Taffy frowned. She couldn't spot an empty table anywhere, either. Oh, well, she thought. Shawnie will be here any minute.

Sliding her tray along in front of the steam table, Taffy selected a taco salad, a brownie, and milk. Then she paid the cashier and stepped aside to look for Shawnie again.

"Where *is* she?" Taffy murmured as she scanned the tables one by one. No Shawnie. She absolutely was not in the cafeteria.

21

What on earth could have happened to her? wondered Taffy. Is it possible that she got sick during class and had to go home? Oh, my gosh. Then who am I going to sit with?

Taffy tried not to panic, but the idea of eating alone on her first day back at Wakeman made little shivers race up her spine. She glanced around for a friendly face as she moved slowly among the tables. Alexis Duvall, Lisa Snow, and Marcie Bee were deep in conversation when she went past their table, and they didn't look up. She could feel Jana Morgan and Katie Shannon's eyes on her as they waited for the rest of The Fabulous Five, but naturally, they didn't invite her to sit with them.

Out of the corner of her eye she saw Cory and his friends at a table near the wall. She would die if he saw her wandering around with no place to sit. Why didn't someone at least speak to her? Suddenly she realized she was heading straight for The Fantastic Foursome, and she made a quick left. The last thing she needed was another run-in with Laura McCall and her friends.

Why wasn't there at least an empty table? Taffy felt her face turning a bright crimson. Her appetite was totally gone, and she was thinking seriously of throwing her lunch into the trash and getting out of the cafeteria before the situation got any more embarrassing when she heard someone call her name.

"Taffy! Over here!"

Taffy frowned when she looked around and saw that

it was Kimm Taylor who was shouting at her. Kimm motioned toward a table near the door that was being vacated by some eighth-graders. "Come on, Taffy. Would you hold the table while Shawnie and I go through the line?"

"Sure," said Taffy as she put her tray down. She glanced at Shawnie, who was nearby, standing at the end of the food line, and asked, "Where have you been?"

"Sorry we're late," said Shawnie. "Kimm and I had to stop in the girls' room for a minute."

Taffy nodded, trying not to let her irritation show. What was Kimm Taylor doing with Shawnie again, anyway? Didn't she realize that Shawnie and Taffy were best friends, and that they hadn't seen each other for six long weeks? "You'd think she'd give us some privacy to catch up," she muttered under her breath.

She was nibbling at her taco salad when the two returned to the table. Shawnie sat down across from Taffy, and Kimm slid in next to Shawnie.

"Remember what I told you last week about how Marcie Bee made such a fool of herself over Derek Travelstead in math class?" Kimm asked Shawnie, who nodded. "Well, you should have seen her today."

"Really? What did she do this time?" asked Shawnie around a bite of tuna salad sandwich.

"Well . . ." Kimm said from behind a hand and looking around in case someone at another table was listening. "She actually passed him a note asking him who he liked and saying that—get this—a *friend* wanted to know."

"You're kidding!" shrieked Shawnie. "What did Derek do?"

"Nothing," replied Kimm. "He just looked at her as if he thought she was nuts. It was hysterical."

Taffy watched the two girls giggle wildly. She had never felt so left out in her life.

"I didn't know Marcie liked Derek," she offered in a weak voice.

"Oh, that all started while you were in Hollywood," Shawnie assured her. "Didn't I write you about it?"

Taffy shook her head.

"Sorry," said Shawnie. "I must have forgotten. But wait till you hear this, Taffy. It's hysterical." Then she turned back to Kimm. "So what did Marcie do then? Freak out?"

"Naw," said Kimm. "The bell rang before she could do anything else. I can't wait till class tomorrow."

As Shawnie and Kimm concentrated on their lunches, Taffy's mind was racing for some way to get into the conversation. Should I tell them more things about Hollywood? No, she thought. Now wasn't the time. Still, she had to think of something. She felt like a total outsider. They could talk all day about things that had happened while she was gone, and there was no way she could join in.

Suddenly an idea popped into her mind. Cory, she thought. That's it!

"Guess what, guys. Cory asked me to go to a movie Friday night," she announced proudly.

"Terrific!" said Shawnie. "We can double-date, the way we planned. Craig asked me, too."

Taffy smiled triumphantly at Kimm. "Shawnie and I decided a long time ago that we wanted to double just as soon as I got home from Hollywood."

Kimm looked thoughtful for a moment and then shrugged. "I'm surprised Cory asked you to a movie," she said. "He's already seen everything playing at Cinema Six."

Taffy's eyes flared in anger. *How do you know?* she wanted to shout. *Just because you sing with his band doesn't mean you know everything about him!* Instead, she said in an icy voice, "Well, *maybe* he doesn't care about that as long as he's with someone he really likes."

If Kimm realized that Taffy was angry, she didn't let on, but Taffy could see Shawnie squirming nervously.

No one said much more during lunch, and Taffy was beginning to wonder if she had been wrong to snap at Kimm. She hadn't meant to make Shawnie mad, just let her know that she wasn't exactly thrilled to have Kimm around all the time. Didn't Shawnie realize that it hurt to come home and find your best friend hanging around with someone else?

4※

"Want to go to Bumpers?" Shawnie asked, stopping by Taffy's locker after school.

Shawnie's big smile perked up Taffy's spirits a little. All afternoon she had been worrying about whether her anger in the cafeteria would make Shawnie change her mind about their friendship.

"Unfortunately, Cory and Craig won't be there," added Shawnie. "I just saw Craig, and he said the band was going to practice."

This time Taffy's spirits soared. That meant Kimm wouldn't be at Bumpers, either.

"In fact," Shawnie went on as Taffy got her books out of her locker, "the band has started using every

27

spare minute to practice. The plan is to sound *big-time* so that they can get more jobs."

"I guess I can identify with that," Taffy admitted as she pulled her jacket off its hook. "On the set we practiced our lines for hours and hours before they rolled the cameras, and sometimes . . ."

Taffy stopped in midsentence. Shawnie was listening with a sort of glazed look in her eyes. Of course she doesn't understand what I'm talking about, Taffy thought. Nobody would who hasn't been on a movie set and seen what happens, and Shawnie's just trying to be polite. She's really more interested in what's going on around good old Wacko. Sighing, Taffy said, "Let's go on to Bumpers. Okay?"

"Sure," said Shawnie. "We'll have to hurry, anyway, if we're going to get a seat." Shouldering her backpack, she fell into step with Taffy, and her eyes began to gleam. "On the way you can tell me more about Raven Blaine. He's so *totally*, *TOTALLY* awesome on the screen, but what's he really like in person?"

"Oh, Shawnie, I wish you could meet him."

"Ditto, I'm sure," Shawnie interjected, and giggled. "Come on. Tell me something secret about him. Did he kiss you?"

Taffy pictured Raven in her mind and answered, "Not yet, but I know he would have if I'd stayed there. Oh, Shawnie, he's so sensitive. Really. I know that's hard to believe, but it's true." She bit her lower lip for a moment, wondering if she should say more, but after all, Shawnie was her best friend. "Promise you won't tell, and I'll tell you his real name."

"You mean Raven Blaine isn't his real name?" exclaimed Shawnie. When Taffy didn't answer, she added, "Okay. Okay. I promise I won't breathe a word to another living soul. Now, tell me everything."

"Well," Taffy began, "his real name is Len Butterworth, and he's totally shy around girls."

"Oh, come on," said Shawnie. "I've seen him on TV. There's nothing shy about him."

"That's because he's playing a part," Taffy insisted. "He can say or do anything when he's acting, but when he's just being himself, he's shy. When he sent me a bouquet of roses, and even this gold star necklace, he was too shy to sign 'Raven' on the card. Instead, he signed 'Len.' I didn't know his real name then, and I thought they were from someone else."

"Wow," said Shawnie, getting a dreamy look on her face. "That's so romantic. I mean, a famous star who likes you so much, he sends you presents but is too shy to sign his name. That sounds like a movie plot."

Taffy opened the door to Bumpers. "I'll tell you more later, okay? And don't forget," she added as she remembered Kimm, "you promised you wouldn't tell *anybody*."

Shawnie nodded, and the two of them began searching for a table.

"Quick!" Shawnie shouted. "Somebody's leaving that bumper car. Grab it."

She was pointing to a green bumper car near the center of the restaurant that two ninth-grade boys were leaving. The bumper cars were relics of an old amusement park ride and were what gave the place its name. Taffy plunked her books in the seat and scooted inside an instant before a group of kids coming from the back of the room could get to it. "Whoa. That was close," she said as Shawnie sat down beside her.

"Oh, hi, Taffy. I heard you were back."

Taffy looked up to see Alexis Duvall and Lisa Snow stopping beside the bumper car. It was Alexis who had spoken, and Taffy couldn't help remembering that neither Alexis nor Lisa had even so much as spoken to her in the cafeteria. Still, she thought, they're being friendly now.

"Hi, guys," Taffy replied. "What's been going on?"

"Absolutely nothing," said Alexis.

"You can say that again," agreed Lisa. "This place is a snore, totally dullsville."

"Gee, you should have been in Hollywood with me," Taffy said eagerly, as a crowd of kids began to gather around the bumper car. "Things were anything but dull." She raised her voice so that everyone could hear. "There were lots of teenagers in the cast, and we went to the beach and did tons of fun things. I even went to a party at the director's Beverly Hills mansion, and Patrick Swayze was there!"

"Big deal," she heard someone mutter.

Taffy winced, knowing the remark had been meant

for her. Someone must be jealous. The rest of the crowd looked interested.

"You probably know some of the other stars in my movie," she went on. "Raven Blaine was in it. He may be one of the biggest stars in the world, but in person he's really kind and sensitive. Paige Kramer was in it, too. Remember her? She used to star in her own weekly TV show called *Daddy's Little Darling*. We got to be terrific friends."

"Wow! It sounds like all your Hollywood friends are better than your friends back here in good old *boring* Wacko!" challenged Tammy Lucero.

"Right," said Marcie Bee. "I'm surprised you'd even sit with Shawnie, now that you have big-deal movie stars for friends."

Taffy looked at them in shock. She opened her mouth to reply, but Shelly Bramlett cut her off.

"Oh, I just *love* my new friends," Shelly said in a falsetto voice, which Taffy knew was supposed to be an imitation of her own voice. "They're all *sooooo* famous!"

Laughter broke out around the room.

"Hey, guys. Wait a minute," Shawnie yelled over the noise, but no one was paying any attention to her. Then turning to Taffy, she said, "Come on. Let's get out of here."

Taffy couldn't speak. She tried to hold back the tears gathering behind her eyes. *What's the matter with everybody?* she wanted to shout. *Why didn't they under-*

stand that she was just explaining about her life in Hollywood? The stars she had met may have been famous, but they were just regular kids.

Picking up her things, she followed Shawnie outside into the refreshing air.

"Oh, Shawnie. Why did they say all those things?" she cried.

Shawnie put an arm around her shoulder. "I guess they think you're bragging, that you think you're better than they are, now that you've made a Hollywood movie."

Taffy was silent for a moment. Then she sighed and looked sadly at Shawnie. "But it just isn't fair," she began. "Can you imagine how awful it is to have something wonderful happen in your life and not be able to talk about it because everyone thinks you're bragging?"

"You can talk to me about it," Shawnie said softly. "I won't think you're bragging."

Taffy looked at the sincere expression on Shawnie's face. Surely Kimm Taylor couldn't wreck their friendship.

"Thanks, Shawnie," said Taffy. "You're a good friend. But I still don't understand what's wrong with everybody else."

"They'll get over it," offered Shawnie. "It's just that nobody from Wakeman Junior High has ever gone off to Hollywood to make a movie before. And hearing about it makes some kids feel like big fat nothings."

Taffy sighed and headed for home. "I don't know

why I bothered to go all the way to Hollywood to film *Nobody Likes Tiffany Stafford*," she whispered to herself. "They could have brought the camera crew here to Wakeman and called the movie *Nobody Likes Taffy Sinclair.*"

When she got home, her mother was waiting for her in the kitchen.

"How did your first day back at school go, dear? Was everybody excited about having a movie star for a classmate?"

Taffy dropped her books on the counter with a thud. "Are you kidding?" she muttered. "Most of them treated me like poison."

Mrs. Sinclair nodded and smiled sympathetically. "I'm sure they're a little jealous. After all, none of them have ever done what you have."

Taffy sighed. "Shawnie says that my going to Hollywood makes them feel like big fat nothings. Do you think that's true?"

"Probably, but you can't let that bother you, sweetheart. You have a wonderful future as an actress, and someday they'll all be bragging that they knew you in school. Just you wait and see."

But what about now? Taffy wanted to ask as she headed upstairs to her room. Someday was a long way away. She thought about what had happened during the day. Her overhearing The Fabulous Five talking behind her back. Laura McCall's pretending to gag and giggling with her friends when Taffy told her homeroom about Hollywood. Taffy's finding out that Kimm Taylor had practically stolen her best friend while she was gone. And now, the scene at Bumpers.

I don't want to wait for someday, she thought miserably. I want kids to like me now.

5❋

For the next couple of days Taffy bit her tongue every time she was tempted to mention Hollywood or Raven Blaine or anything else about making a movie. It was more difficult than she had expected, but it was the only solution she could come up with to keep people from thinking she was bragging.

She sighed every time she looked at her bulletin board at the clipping from the Hollywood newspaper of her and Raven Blaine, or at the gold star necklace that Raven had given her. But she didn't wear the necklace to school again. It would just remind me of things that I'm better off not thinking about, she told herself.

On Friday Cory asked if he could walk her home after school so they could make plans for their date that evening. Before they had even left the school grounds, Cory had told her that he would come by at six-thirty and that they would be doubling with Shawnie and Craig.

With that settled Taffy linked arms with Cory for the rest of the walk home, sauntering along as slowly as possible. She wanted to make the time with him last, even though she knew her mother would be sitting in the car in the Sinclair driveway, impatiently tapping her fingertips against the steering wheel and watching the hands on her wristwatch move closer to the time Taffy's acting lesson was to begin.

"You're awfully quiet. What are you thinking about?" asked Cory. "I hope it's not Raven Blaine."

"Raven Blaine!" Taffy echoed. Her heart began to pound. "Why would I be thinking about him?"

Cory looked down at her, a tiny frown creasing his face. "I heard that you told everybody at Bumpers a few days ago that Raven Blaine was totally cool."

"That's not what I said," Taffy argued. "I never ever said he was totally cool. What I said was that he was a really nice person, that's all."

"Okay, okay," said Cory. "I didn't mean to come off sounding jealous."

"That's okay," said Taffy, but her heart was still pounding. Did Cory suspect how she felt about Raven?

"So, what were you thinking about?" he asked.

Taffy squinted up at Cory in the bright sunlight. "I

was just dreading going to my acting class," she said. "My mother is determined to make me into an actress."

"I thought you liked acting," said Cory.

"Don't get me wrong. I do like acting, but I'd also like to have more time for other things—" she flashed him a big smile—"like spending time with you. It'll never happen, though. Now that the producers of *Nobody Likes Tiffany Stafford* are considering turning it into a weekly television series, my mother's more determined than ever. I don't know what she'd do if they cast someone else in the part of Tiffany Stafford."

Cory stopped in the middle of the sidewalk. "Do you mean that you might go back to Hollywood?" he asked incredulously.

Taffy didn't say anything for a moment. She hadn't wanted to tell Cory about that possibility, but it had slipped out. "Maybe," she admitted, "but I really don't want to. Honest. It's my mother who wants it. She's devoting her whole life to making me a star." Taffy hoped her voice sounded sincere. She hadn't lied to Cory. Not exactly, anyway. Part of her did want to stay here and be a real teenager. But even though she couldn't admit it to him, part of her loved the glamorous life in Hollywood and wanted to return.

"If you're going to take lessons, why don't you take singing lessons?" suggested Cory. "Then you could take Kimm Taylor's place as singer for The Dreadful Alternatives."

"Replace Kimm? You've got to be kidding," said Taffy. "But then . . ." she mused, and lapsed into thought. Maybe that wouldn't be such a bad idea. Shawnie had said that the band was trying hard to make it big. If that happened, she wanted herself—not Kimm—to be in on the glory. Besides, it would serve Kimm right for trying to steal her best friend.

"I'm serious," said Cory. "Talk to your mom. Tell her that you'd rather be a singer. She ought to go for that, since you could still be a star. You don't have to mention The Dreadful Alternatives."

"I wouldn't dare ask her anything like that," Taffy said with a laugh. "She'd come totally unglued."

"What would your dad say?" Cory asked. "Would he be more sympathetic?"

Taffy shook her head. "It wouldn't do any good if he was. He wasn't a Radio City Music Hall Rockette who gave up a career for marriage and a family. Mother considers herself the authority on show business, and she makes all those kinds of decisions."

Just as Taffy had predicted, Mrs. Sinclair sat idling the car at the bottom of the driveway. When she saw Taffy and Cory approaching, she jumped out and began waving.

"Hurry, Taffy. Do you know what time it is? We're going to be late."

Taffy looked at Cory helplessly. "I have to go," she whispered.

Cory glanced quickly toward Mrs. Sinclair, who

was ducking back into the car, and then pretended to cough. When he put his hand to his mouth, he kissed the tip of his index finger and brushed the finger across Taffy's cheek.

"See you later," he said softly.

Taffy smiled and nodded as she got into her car. She touched the spot where Cory had left the kiss as she waved good-bye to him. He was so wonderful.

Who knows about Raven Blaine? she thought. He seemed to care about me. But maybe he acts that way to every girl he meets.

She sighed and thought about Cory again, closing her eyes and seeing them together on stage with The Dreadful Alternatives. Now, more than ever, she wanted to be a regular person, an ordinary seventh-grader at Wakeman Junior High, instead of a movie star. And maybe someday The Dreadful Alternatives, with her as their singer, would make it into the big time. Then she would be a star after all.

"Taffy. Did you hear me?" asked her mother as she pulled into a parking space in front of a red brick building. "I asked if you've memorized the scenes your class is going to work on today."

Taffy blinked away her daydreams. "I read them over a few times," she offered.

Mrs. Sinclair shook her head. "I certainly hope you don't embarrass yourself," she scolded. "I'd think the least you could do is memorize your scenes. Well, come on."

Why won't she leave me alone? Taffy wondered miserably as she followed her mother into the building and up the stairs. Why won't she just let me lead my own life the way I want to?

Taffy thought about mentioning the idea of taking singing lessons instead of acting lessons, but she knew the timing wasn't right. Maybe she could bring up the subject another time, when her mother was in a better mood. But she would have to be careful and handle it just right. The chance to replace Kimm was too important to make a mistake.

Mrs. Sinclair opened the door to The Merry Chase Studio and pushed Taffy in ahead of herself. The walls were covered with pictures of famous actors and actresses who had studied with Merry Chase. Taffy went past the secretary's desk into the room where class was held. It was a large room with twenty-five or thirty chairs lined up in three rows at one end. The rest of the room served as the stage, where the students practiced their roles.

At least a dozen other boys and girls around Taffy's age were already seated. Most sat beside their mothers, but a few others—the lucky ones, to Taffy's way of thinking—were clustered in the third row, talking and giggling together. Taffy looked longingly at this group as her mother tugged at her and pointed to two seats at the front.

When everyone was finally settled, Merry Chase herself took center stage. She was stick-thin with heavy makeup and hair dyed black. Her hair was piled on her head, and she was dressed in a long, flowing muumuu with tons of silver jewelry hanging around her neck.

"Good afternoon, loves," she called out in a deep, throaty voice.

"Good afternoon, Merry Chase," the students answered obediently.

Merry Chase smiled benevolently. "I hope everyone has memorized the scenes for today, because we all want to work hard and become famous movie stars."

Mrs. Sinclair nudged Taffy and looked down her nose at her as if to say, "I told you so!"

Taffy rolled her eyes toward the ceiling and groaned inwardly. She was trapped.

6❋

The telephone was ringing when Taffy got home from acting class.

"Hi, Taffy. It's Cory. How would you feel about going roller-skating instead of to a movie? A lot of kids from Wacko are going to Skateland over on Lincoln Avenue tonight. I thought it might be fun to go along."

"Wow," said Taffy. "I haven't been skating in ages. I'd definitely like to go."

"Great. I'll see you at six-thirty then. And Taffy . . . " He hesitated a moment. "Did you say anything to your mother about singing lessons?"

Taffy bit her lower lip. There was no way she could ever talk her mother into letting her take singing lessons instead of acting lessons, but she didn't want to tell that to Cory. "Not yet," she said.

Stalling wasn't much better than lying, she told herself after they hung up, but it would give her time to plan what to say when Cory asked again. She didn't want to say anything that would make him mad at her, not right now, when they were beginning to date again.

"Remember to be home on time," her mother warned when Taffy came downstairs to wait for Cory that evening. "You need your beauty sleep. What if you get a call to go back to Hollywood and you have dark circles under your eyes?"

"Mo-*ther*!" Taffy said with a huge sigh. "I've never had dark circles under my eyes in my life."

Before Mrs. Sinclair could reply, the doorbell rang. Taffy hurried to open the door and drew in her breath at the sight of Cory. He looked so handsome standing there, his blond hair falling gently over his forehead.

"Hello, Cory," her mother said behind her. Then the tone of her voice changed. "Why are you carrying skates? I thought you two were going to a movie."

Taffy winced as she noticed that a pair of black-and-neon-green roller skates were slung over Cory's shoulder. "We changed our minds, Mother. I forgot to tell you."

She could see storm clouds gathering in her mother's eyes.

"A bunch of Wakeman kids are going," she added quickly. "I'll still be home early."

"Taffy! You know you can't go skating. What if you broke a leg? It would *ruin* your movie career!"

Taffy felt as if her whole body were crashing inward. She didn't dare look at Cory. What could she say?

"It's okay, Mrs. Sinclair," said Cory. "We can go to a movie. I guess I wasn't thinking when I asked her to go skating."

In exasperation Taffy spun around and opened her mouth to plead with her mother, but the look of determination on Mrs. Sinclair's face stopped her.

"Come on, Taffy," Cory urged. "It's okay. Honest."

Taffy got her jacket from the hall closet and said good-night to her parents. Then she followed Cory out of the house.

"I feel just awful," she said as they walked down the street toward Cinema Six. "Were we supposed to meet Shawnie and Craig at Skateland?"

Cory nodded. "Don't worry, though. We'll explain later. They'll understand."

Even though Cory seemed perfectly content to see a movie, Taffy couldn't help wishing they could have gone to Skateland. There would be so many Wakeman kids there, and maybe if they saw her with Cory, they would realize that she was just one of them. Maybe they would even forget to hate her for being a movie star. Also, hadn't Kimm said that Cory had already seen all of the movies playing at Cinema Six? No wonder he wanted to skate, she thought. He's probably bored to death.

But halfway through the movie he reached for her hand, and on the way out of the theater he slipped his arm around her waist. "Do you mind if we skip Bumpers tonight?" he said. "There's something I'd like to ask you—in private."

Taffy's eyes widened, and her heart skipped a beat. "It's okay with me," she assured him.

When they were outside, Cory steered her into a small park and motioned toward a bench underneath a beautiful oak tree. They sat down, and he made circles in the dirt with the toe of his sneaker. Finally he looked up and said, "I'll bet things seem pretty dull here after Hollywood, don't they?"

"No, honest," Taffy insisted. "I'm really glad to be back." Then she added quickly, "Going to classes at Wacko is a lot more fun than sitting around with a tutor on a movie set. Of course, we only had to go to school three hours a day, which was pretty neat, but—" She broke off the sentence quickly, embarrassed that she had forgotten her vow not to make a big deal about Hollywood or starring in a movie. She would just answer people's questions and let it go at that. Now she had broken that promise to herself. What if she had blown Cory's feelings for her, too? she thought frantically.

"Yeah. Well, I guess things are different there," Cory said lamely.

"No . . . I mean, yes . . . I mean . . ." she fumbled, trying desperately to think of the right thing to say.

Then, to her surprise, Cory looked at her and said, "I . . . I really missed you while you were in Hollywood."

Taffy felt a pink glow spread over her cheeks. "I missed you, too," she said shyly.

"I was worried that you might like it so much out there that you'd never come back."

Taffy bit her lower lip. She could never admit to Cory just how much she had liked Hollywood and how much she missed it, now that she was home.

"But I did come back," she told him.

"Yeah." Cory grinned broadly. "And am I glad!" He looked down again, making more circles in the dirt with the toe of his sneaker. "What I wanted to know is . . ." he began, ". . . would you go steady with me?"

Taffy's heart leapt into her throat. Had she heard him right? Had he actually asked her to go steady? But the look in his eyes told her that he had.

"I mean, if you don't want to, or if you think you're going back to Hollywood . . ."

"Oh, yes," she answered quickly. "I'd love to go steady with you."

Cory leaned toward her and kissed her softly on the lips.

I'll never go back to Hollywood, she vowed silently as they walked toward home. And I'll talk my mother into letting me take singing lessons so I can sing with Cory's band, if it's the last thing I do.

7*

The next day was Saturday, and as soon as Taffy finished breakfast, she raced to the phone to call Shawnie and tell her the big news, that Cory had asked her to go steady. She also wanted to explain why they hadn't been at the skating rink. Taffy let the phone ring at least a dozen times, but no one answered.

"Rats!" she said in frustration. She knew Shawnie and her mother frequently went shopping on Saturday. It was obvious from Shawnie's fabulous wardrobe. But she was still disappointed. It was the same old thing, she thought, good news and no one to tell it to.

She wandered around the house all morning, alternating between trying Shawnie's number again and daydreaming about Cory and how wonderful it would be to be onstage with him.

She was stretched across her bed, picturing her favorite scene for the hundredth time. The setting was the Wakeman Junior High gymnasium. The Dreadful Alternatives, with her as singer, were performing onstage. On the gym floor the crowd was applauding wildly. Suddenly a knock on her bedroom door jolted her back to reality.

"Taffy?" her mother called from the hallway. "May I come in? I have something for you."

"Sure," Taffy answered, wondering why her mother sounded so excited.

Mrs. Sinclair entered the room smiling broadly and handed a letter to Taffy. "This just came for you. It's from your friend Paige Kramer in Hollywood."

Taffy drew in her breath. "From Paige?" she asked excitedly. "Gosh, thanks."

Paige Kramer was a former child star. At first she had been Taffy's enemy on the movie set because she had wanted the starring role that Taffy got. But later, after Taffy had gotten to know Paige and understand her problems, they had become best friends. Taffy carried the letter to her bed and sat cross-legged in the center. She started to open it when she noticed that her mother had not moved. Mrs. Sinclair was watching her intently.

"Hurry, Taffy, open it," her mother instructed.

"Paige might have heard whether or not your movie is going to become a TV series."

Taffy frowned. It was her letter. Her *private* letter.

"I'll let you know if she says anything about it," said Taffy. She put the letter in her lap and looked at her mother calmly.

"Well!" huffed Mrs. Sinclair. Then she hurried out of the room, muttering. "After all, I *am* your mother."

As soon as the door closed again, Taffy sank back against her pillows and eagerly tore open the envelope.

Dear Taffy,

I know you've only been gone a few days, but I had to write anyway, to tell you how much I miss you. KJ, Tess, Raven, and I went to the beach yesterday. Raven wore his red wig and sunglasses disguise so he wouldn't be mobbed by teenage girls, but things just weren't the same without you.

I've also been wondering how you're getting along at school. How is everyone treating you? Okay, I hope. Remember, I know how tough it can be when everyone is jealous.

We're all keeping our fingers crossed that the producers will decide to go ahead with the TV series so that you'll be back here soon. There is supposed to be a decision

*in a few weeks. I'll let you know as soon as I hear any-
thing. Write soon.*

*Love,
Paige*

*P.S. I almost forgot! Raven asked for your address! He
said he's going to write to you really soon!*

The words in the letter hit Taffy like a tidal wave.
She swallowed hard and read them again. *Things just
weren't the same without you. . . . We're all keeping our
fingers crossed . . . that you'll be back here soon. . . .* But
most of all her eyes kept going back to the last two lines
of the letter.

*I almost forgot! Raven asked for your address! He said
he's going to write to you really soon!*

Taffy felt as if someone were squeezing her heart.
Hollywood had been so much fun, so exciting compared to Wakeman Junior High. She was trying to fit
in. And she really did like Cory, but . . . did Raven
really care about her, too?

"Oh, why did this letter have to come now?" she
whispered.

She heard the telephone ringing downstairs, and a
moment later her mother called up to her.

"It's for you, Taffy."

Taffy folded the letter and put it under her pillow.
Then she raced for the phone.

"Hi, Taffy," said Shawnie as soon as Taffy said hello.

"Oh, hi," Taffy answered in surprise. "I've been trying to call you all morning. Did you and your mom go shopping?"

"No," said Shawnie. "I was over at Kimm's. I left a sweater over there last week, and I went by to pick it up."

"Oh," replied Taffy in a small voice.

"I love going over to Kimm's," Shawnie continued. "Her house is decorated with all this neat Oriental stuff. I even learned to eat with chopsticks there."

"Great," Taffy said sarcastically. Why couldn't Shawnie understand how it made her feel to hear about Kimm all the time when Shawnie was supposed to be *her* best friend?

"Hey, the reason I called was to find out where you and Cory were last night. Is everything okay?"

"Sure, everything's great," Taffy assured her. "We went to a movie instead of Skateland."

"What?"

"My mom wouldn't let me go skating. She was afraid that I'd break my leg and ruin my acting career." Taffy groaned.

Shawnie giggled. "Oh, no! That's too wild. So did you guys have a good time?"

"Did we ever," said Taffy, forgetting for the moment about Kimm and about Paige's letter. "You'll never guess what happened after the movie. Cory asked me to go steady."

"Wow!" shouted Shawnie. "That's super! What did he say? Tell me everything."

Taffy closed her eyes. "Well . . ." she began, and told Shawnie all about it, not leaving out a single detail. "I couldn't *believe* it," she added happily.

"And when you first got home from Hollywood, you were worried that he didn't like you anymore. See? What did I tell you? He's crazy about you," Shawnie said. "So I guess you'll forget all about Raven Blaine now, right?"

Shawnie's question startled Taffy. "Oh . . . well, sure . . . I guess so," she fumbled.

"He's awfully far away, anyway," Shawnie offered.

"Right," agreed Taffy, sounding more convinced than she felt. "I mean, I'll probably never see him again."

But what do I really mean? thought Taffy as she hung up the phone. She had never felt so totally confused before. She went back to her room and pulled Paige's letter out from under her pillow, then read it once again.

I like Cory a lot, she thought. And I do want to go steady with him and fit in at Wakeman. But *can* I fit in? My best friend spends half her time with someone else. And I can't seem to forget Hollywood and Raven Blaine.

❂   ❂   ❂

For the next few days, Taffy raced home every day and checked the mail for a letter from Raven. Every day she was disappointed. At first she made up excuses for why he hadn't written.

He's busy. But Paige had written they went to the beach. If he had time to do that, surely he had time for a letter.

He's lost my address. But if he got it from Paige in the first place, he could get it from her again.

Finally there was only one reason she could think of for not hearing from Raven. *He doesn't like me after all*, she decided.

8*

Gradually life at Wakeman Junior High got back to normal for Taffy. Most kids seemed to forget that she was a movie star, and they stopped staring at her in the halls and whispering behind her back. Word had spread quickly that she and Cory were going steady, and now she was sure that the jealous looks she got from other girls were because she was Cory Dillon's girlfriend.

Still, she couldn't help feeling a little depressed at how ordinary life at Wakeman was after the excitement of the movie set.

"It's so boring. All I do is go to the same old classes at the same old times day after day," she complained to Shawnie one day at lunch. "At least when I had a tutor on the set, I could work on whichever subject I felt like at the moment, just as long as I got it all done. And I only had to spend three hours a day in school. The rest of the time I rehearsed with the other kids or shot the scenes. It was definitely a lot more fun."

Shawnie nodded. "It does get pretty boring here sometimes," she admitted. "If it weren't for Media Club, I'd go berserk." Shawnie put down the sandwich she had started to bite into and looked at Taffy. "Hey, I've got a great idea. Why don't you join Media Club?"

"Media Club?" Taffy echoed. "Why would I want to do that?"

"What do you mean, *why*?" asked Shawnie. "You already know that we're doing a weekly show on the local cable television station. It's called *The Wakeman Bulletin Board*. If you got involved, it would give you a chance to get back in front of a camera again. You'd love it. Besides, it's something we could have a blast doing together."

Taffy gave Shawnie a skeptical look.

"I can see it all now," said Shawnie, bubbling with enthusiasm. "The greatest show biz team of all time: Pendergast and Sinclair. Ta-DA! Whoops!" she added, laughing, "*Sinclair* and Pendergast, of course."

Taffy smiled, but then her face clouded. "I don't know," she said slowly. "It wouldn't be anything like Hollywood."

"Of course not," Shawnie conceded. "But it's fun

anyway. And with your experience, I'll bet there's a lot you could teach us—Mr. Levine included."

Interest flickered in Taffy's mind. She hadn't thought of it that way. It would be fun explaining to everyone how movies are made. She might even be able to suggest ways to improve the TV show.

"Come on, Taffy, say you'll do it," pleaded Shawnie. "Come with me today. We're going to be filming this week's show."

"Well . . ." Taffy hesitated.

"Pleeeease," said Shawnie, clasping her hands in front of her as if she were begging.

"Okay," said Taffy. "I'll try it once."

The more Taffy thought about Media Club during her afternoon classes, the better it sounded. Producing a television show would be a lot more interesting than math or English. And Shawnie had been right when she'd said it was something fun that they could do together.

After school Taffy met Shawnie at her locker.

"The club meets in the media center," said Shawnie as she led Taffy through the halls. "This month I'm one of the reporters, so I won't be in front of the camera."

"*On* camera," Taffy corrected.

"Yeah, sure. Whatever you say," said Shawnie with an embarrassed laugh.

All conversation stopped when Taffy walked into

the media center. Funny Hawthorne and Beth Barry were moving chairs around, and they froze and stared at her. Shane Arrington and Jon Smith had been standing to one side talking, and they looked up, too.

Paul Smoke was the first to speak. "Oh, hi, Taffy. We're fixing up the set so that we can film today."

"You mean, you're *dressing* the set," said Taffy. "That's what we call it in Hollywood."

Her words were met with stony silence. Oh, no, she thought. I'm doing it again. I'm talking about Hollywood and and turning everyone off. Still, she thought stubbornly, I know what I'm talking about. I thought that the purpose of this club was to learn about things like that.

"Come on, Taffy," said Shawnie, tugging on her arm. "Let me show you around."

"I know everyone resents me," she whispered to Shawnie. "Did you see the looks on Beth's and Funny's faces?"

"Don't worry about it," Shawnie assured her. "They'll get over it when they see what a pro you are."

Taffy wasn't sure they would, but she sighed and followed Shawnie on her grand tour.

"Jon suggested this corner of the media center as our set," Shawnie continued. "We think it looks a lot like the *Today* show or *Good Morning America*, don't you?"

Taffy looked at Shawnie in disbelief, but she didn't reply.

"And that big posterboard on the easel is the title for

our show. The camera zooms in on it at the beginning of each program. We had it professionally lettered. Doesn't it look great?"

Taffy nodded mutely. The Media Club was far more *un*professional than she could ever have imagined.

"Well, hello, Taffy," said Mr. Levine. He had been looking over the script when the girls approached, and now he glanced up and smiled cordially.

Before Taffy could return his greeting, Shawnie said, "Taffy wants to join Media Club. Isn't that great? She'll be able to teach us all kinds of things."

Taffy was sure she heard someone groan behind her, but she pretended not to notice.

"We're certainly glad to have you," said Mr. Levine. "You might just want to watch today and see how we run our operation."

Shawnie pulled over a chair that had been moved off the set and motioned for Taffy to sit down, then perched on the arm beside her. "Paul Smoke and Tim Riggs are co-anchors, and Beth's the director this month. I was director last month. It's a hard job, but it's fun to boss everybody around," she said, giggling.

Taffy narrowed her eyes and watched Beth motion for Paul to scoot his chair a little closer to Tim's. Some director, she thought. Beth doesn't know the first thing about the job. *My* director, Jerry Lowenthal, would have noticed right away that half of Paul's face will be in shadows. She glanced toward Jon Smith, blinking in amazement when she noticed that he was focusing an ordinary camcorder that rested on his shoulder.

"He's filming with *that*?" she asked in astonishment.

"Hey," Shawnie protested. "This is a low-budget show."

"But . . . but . . ." Taffy sputtered. She was picturing the set of *Nobody Likes Tiffany Stafford*, where massive cameras moved around on wheels, and the lighting equipment and reflectors created the right mix of lights and shadows, and the sound booms were carefully placed to pick up the slightest noise.

"Where are the gaffers and the grips?" she wondered out loud. "Aren't you going to block out the movements of the cast?"

"Gaffers and grips? What are those? Jokes and props?" asked Shane, and everyone laughed.

Everyone but Taffy. She could feel her face turning bright crimson. She knew everyone was watching her, so she took a deep breath and said as calmly as she could, "Gaffers are the people in charge of the lighting equipment, and grips are the workmen who move it around."

"And I suppose that blocking out the movements of the cast is like blocking out football plays?" said Tim.

"Right," confirmed Taffy, glad that at least one person knew what she was talking about. "It's really important so everyone feels comfortable on the set before the cameras roll."

"Well, this isn't *exactly* Hollywood," Beth said sarcastically.

You can say that again, Taffy thought, but she didn't

say it. Instead she looked around at the corner of the junior high media center that was doubling as the set, and at the hand-held camcorder Jon was going to use to film the show, and at her old enemy Beth Barry—the director—who knew absolutely nothing about directing, and her heart dropped into her shoes.

"No," she whispered to herself, "this really isn't Hollywood *at all*."

9✣

"*I* just couldn't believe how amateurish the whole thing was," Taffy complained for the hundredth time. She was talking to Cory on the telephone and had spent the past ten minutes filling him in on the after-school Media Club meeting she had gone to.

"So don't join," said Cory. "After all, you're big-time. You don't owe them anything."

"I know," Taffy said slowly. She twisted the phone cord around a finger and considered. "But it might hurt Shawnie's feelings if I don't join, and there really is a lot I could teach them. I'm going to think it over some more before I decide."

"In the meantime, why not come over to my house Saturday afternoon and listen to The Dreadful Alternatives rehearse," offered Cory. "We won't tell Kimm why you're really there," he added with a sly laugh.

A thrill raced through Taffy. Singing with Cory's band couldn't compare to Hollywood, but it would be a lot more fun than the Media Club.

"But what about Kimm?" she wondered aloud. "And the guys, too? Won't they think it's a little funny that I'm there?"

"Naw," Cory assured her. "Craig usually invites Shawnie to rehearsals on Saturdays. That's how Shawnie and Kimm got to be friends."

So that was it, Taffy thought, frowning. She had wondered how the two of them had gotten so friendly while she was in Hollywood. Keeping an eye on Kimm was another good reason for her to accept Cory's invitation.

"I'd love to go," said Taffy, "and if Shawnie's going, we'll ride over together on our bikes."

Shawnie was ecstatic at school the next morning when Taffy mentioned she'd be going to the rehearsal that Saturday. "That's terrific," she cried. "I knew he'd ask you to come. You won't believe how much fun the rehearsals are."

"I'll come by for you on my bike," Taffy volunteered.

"Great," said Shawnie. "Then we can ride over and get Kimm."

Anger flared in Taffy for an instant, but she tried

not to let it show. She didn't want Shawnie to know she was jealous.

"You like Kimm a lot, don't you?" she asked cautiously.

Shawnie nodded. "So will you when you get to know her better. She's really nice, and besides that, she's . . . well, she's interesting."

"She seems like an ordinary person to me," Taffy grumbled.

Shawnie thought for a moment. "She is an ordinary person. At school she seems like everybody else. But didn't I tell you that one of her grandmothers came to this country from China and I learned to eat with chopsticks at her house? I've never known anyone like her before. She's fun to be around. Just wait, you'll see."

Taffy was glad that the bell rang then. They headed for their lockers, Taffy trying to figure out why Shawnie thought Kimm was so fascinating. So what if she was partly Chinese and ate with chopsticks at home? What had she ever done that was as special as making a movie? Maybe going by for Kimm on Saturday was a good idea after all, Taffy decided. It would give her a chance to look Kimm over more closely.

❀   ❀   ❀

When the phone rang Saturday morning, Taffy heard her mother answer it and then continue talking. Disappointed that it wasn't for her, she started upstairs to her room but stopped midway when she heard her mother calling her.

"Taffy, honey. Good news. Merry Chase is holding a special acting class this afternoon, and she said you absolutely have to be there. Channing Crandall is in town, and he's going to be there, too! Isn't that wonderful?"

Taffy blinked in surprise. Channing Crandall was the Hollywood casting director who had auditioned her for the starring role in *Nobody Likes Tiffany Stafford*. What on earth was he doing in town?

Before she could ask, her mother went on, "I'll bet he has news about the TV series. Won't it be wonderful if he wants you to come back to Hollywood right away?"

Taffy nodded, but deep inside she wasn't sure. She missed Hollywood terribly, but things were going so well here now that . . . *Cory!* Taffy jumped as if she had been stuck with a pin. How could she have forgotten about Cory and about going to The Dreadful Alternatives' rehearsal this afternoon?

"Mom, I'm—"

"You'll have to forget about any plans you have with your friends this afternoon," Mrs. Sinclair interrupted as if she had read Taffy's mind. "This is *much* too important."

Taffy raced up to her room and slammed the door behind her, sprawling across her bed. She needed time to think. What if there was going to be a television series based on the movie? And what if *she* was chosen to play Tiffany Stafford again? It would mean living half the year in Hollywood and half the year at home.

"I almost lost my best friend when I was gone for only six weeks," she said aloud. "What would happen if I left for six *months*?"

She closed her eyes tightly and pulled the pillow over her head, not wanting to think about such a possibility.

"On the other hand," she argued a moment later, tossing the pillow aside and sitting up, "maybe Channing Crandall just happened to be in this part of the country and decided to stop in and say hello. After all, he travels all over the United States looking for talented actors and actresses."

Reluctantly Taffy went to the phone and called Cory, telling him she would have to miss his rehearsal.

"It's some kind of special acting class," she explained, being careful not to mention Channing Crandall or what his presence might mean. "I have to go. Mother laid down the law. Maybe I can come to rehearsal next Saturday," she added hopefully.

"Sure," Cory said without much enthusiasm.

Next Taffy called Shawnie, giving her the same story.

"Gosh, that's too bad," said Shawnie. "I know you would have had a blast. I guess Kimm and I will have to go without you."

Taffy started to say good-bye, but Shawnie spoke again.

"Are you sure you can't get out of going to acting class?" she asked.

"Positive," said Taffy. "Why?"

"Well," Shawnie said slowly, "I may be wrong, but I think that Kimm has a crush on Cory."

Taffy put down the receiver a moment later and stared into space. Now what am I going to do? she thought.

10❋

*T*affy climbed into the car beside her mother and slumped against the door. She stared out the window, but she didn't really see anything. She was thinking about her conversation with Shawnie. What if Shawnie was right about Kimm's crush on Cory? What did Cory think of Kimm? Was he as fascinated with her as Shawnie was? Kimm certainly was pretty with her long, dark hair and her almond-shaped eyes. Anything could happen between Cory and Kimm if Taffy had to return to Hollywood for six long months.

When Taffy and her mother arrived at The Merry Chase Acting Studio, Channing Crandall was standing at the front of the classroom conferring with Merry Chase. He had silver hair and a California tan, and he wore large diamond rings on both hands and a heavy gold chain on one wrist.

"Hello, Taffy," he called out.

Just as Taffy started to return his greeting, her mother rushed forward and began shaking his hand. "Oh, Mr. Crandall, it's so good to see you again," she gushed. "Is it possible that you have some good news for us today?"

Taffy looked around in embarrassment. Why did her mother always have to make a big scene? The other boys and girls had stopped their talking, and everyone was looking at her mother and Channing Crandall.

"Come on, Mother," she urged. "Let's sit down."

"It's all right, Taffy," said the casting director. "I understand your mother's concern. As a matter of fact, things look good for the TV series. We'll know definitely in a couple of weeks, as soon as the movie is shown on television."

"Oh, thank you, Mr. Crandall. Thank you so much," said Mrs. Sinclair.

Just then Merry Chase raised her hand for quiet, and Taffy and her mother found seats.

"Good afternoon, loves," said Merry Chase in her deep, throaty voice.

"Good afternoon, Merry Chase," called out the students.

Taffy sighed. It was always the same.

"I'm sure all of you recognize Channing Crandall, the casting director from Hollywood who was here a few months ago and auditioned our own Taffy Sinclair for her movie role," said Merry Chase.

A ripple of excitement flowed through the crowd.

Merry Chase pierced the air with a blood red fingernail, signaling quiet, and went on. "He's here today looking for more talented boys and girls, because if *Nobody Likes Tiffany Stafford* does become a television series, there will be room for more actresses and actors in the cast. He'd like to see each of you perform."

All around her kids were going bananas. Most of the girls had whipped out brushes and were frantically working on their hair. Others ducked behind the seats in front of them to peek into mirrors and apply eye shadow or lipstick. The boys were mostly horsing around and acting like jerks—as usual, thought Taffy.

Beside her, Mrs. Sinclair squirmed nervously. "I don't understand what's going on here. He wouldn't *dare* replace you in the starring role of Tiffany Stafford," she whispered angrily.

"Merry Chase said he's just looking for more kids to fill other roles," said Taffy with a trace of annoyance at her mother. "Naturally a TV series would have a bigger cast than a movie."

"Humph. I certainly hope that's what it is," grumped Mrs. Sinclair.

Taffy scrunched down in her chair. She had never considered the possibility of losing her starring role. What if she blew this audition on purpose and Mr. Crandall picked someone else?

At least then I wouldn't have to leave home again just when I'm starting to fit in, she thought. I could keep my best friend and my boyfriend. And I could replace Kimm as the band's singer. The idea seemed suddenly appealing.

Channing Crandall moved to the center of the stage. "Boys and girls," he said in a booming voice, "so that I may see each of you at your best, I'm going to ask you to do some improvisation. Who can tell me what improvisation is?"

Hands shot up all over the room, but Mr. Crandall chose an especially pretty brunette in the front row named Summer Lacey. Taffy had never liked Summer. She was too conceited. Taffy would die if Summer stole her part.

Summer stood and flashed a big smile at the casting director as she told him her name. "Improvisation is acting without a script," she said importantly. "It's making up the story and the lines as you go along."

"Thank you, Summer. That's exactly right," said Mr. Crandall. "Improvisation lets you use your imagination to the fullest. I'm sure Merry Chase has told you the importance of imagination in *becoming* the character you're playing."

Kids nodded all around the room. Taffy bit her lower lip and thought about how easy it would be to improvise poorly. Then perhaps Channing Crandall would decide to cast someone else in the role of Tiffany Stafford. She stole a glance at her mother, sitting beside her, and thought about how disappointed she would be. She would just have to understand, Taffy thought stubbornly.

"Summer, since you're already standing, won't you go first?" asked Channing Crandall.

Some of the color drained out of Summer's face, and Taffy thought she saw her flinch slightly at his words. It was awful to be first, and Taffy almost felt sorry for her. Nodding slightly, Summer went to the front of the room.

The casting director rested his chin in his hand and looked at her pensively for a moment. "You are a baby-sitter," he began, waving a finger in the air as an orchestra conductor waves a baton. "You are caring for three preschoolers who are each trying to get into mischief."

Giggles rippled through the room.

"One is getting into the refrigerator. Another is climbing up the front of the cupboards. And the third has the cat by the tail. The phone rings. It's the children's mother. You must stop all three disasters while talking to her and not let on to her that things are out of control." He paused for Summer to visualize the scene and then gave the signal for her to begin.

Summer looked flustered for a moment. Then she began swatting the air around her ankles and grabbing for imaginary children as she kept a pretend telephone receiver clamped between her shoulder and her ear.

"Hello, Mrs. Jones," she said. "Yes, everything's

fine. The little angels are behaving perfectly. In fact, they're coloring a picture for you right now."

Watching in amusement as Summer continued to improvise, Taffy joined in the applause when Mr. Crandall indicated she could return to her seat. Summer was good. Very good. Taffy felt little prickles of jealousy creep up the back of her neck at all the attention Summer was getting. Even some of the mothers were congratulating her on a good job.

Next Mr. Crandall called Cynthia Cameron to the front of the room. Tall, blond Cynthia was Taffy's biggest rival for modeling jobs and had almost stolen a television commercial away from Taffy last spring when Taffy had been too busy trying to recover her lost diary to attend an audition. What if Cynthia got my role in the television series? Taffy thought in horror.

Taffy narrowed her eyes and watched Cynthia improvise for the casting director. He told her that she was alone in a burning building. There was only one way out, through a window, and the flames were quickly closing in on that window. But she couldn't escape yet. Fido, the dog she had loved all her life, was still somewhere in the burning house.

Cynthia began swatting at the flames and smoke and calling out to Fido. She looked under imaginary furniture and then toward her shrinking escape route with an expression of terror on her face.

She's good, too, thought Taffy. Terrific, as a matter of fact.

When Cynthia finished her scene, the applause was even louder than it had been for Summer. Taffy made a face as she watched both girls. Summer looked so superior that anyone would think she was already a star. Well, she isn't, thought Taffy. *I* am.

Cynthia was smiling and batting her long eyelashes at Channing Crandall as if he were the most wonderful person on earth.

"It's disgusting," Taffy whispered to herself. "Totally disgusting!"

When the room grew quiet again, the casting director turned to her. "Taffy, we all know what a good actress you are. I'd like for you to show the rest of the class how you do improvisation."

Taffy didn't move for a moment. This was it, the moment when she would have to decide if she wanted to stay at Wacko Junior High and let someone else become a star in her place or if she wanted to prove again to Channing Crandall and everyone in the room, especially Summer and Cynthia, what a terrific actress she was.

"Go on, honey," urged her mother. "What are you waiting for? Break a leg."

Cynthia Cameron put a hand over her mouth to deflect the sound and began imitating Mrs. Sinclair. "Go on, honey. Break your neck."

Giggles broke out all around Cynthia, and Taffy felt the anger rising in her face. Now she certainly couldn't blow her improvisation and let Cynthia make a fool out of her. Tiffany was *her* part.

Taffy raised her head and smiled as she stepped to the front of the room. "I'd be happy to improvise for you, Mr. Crandall," she said demurely, and immediately the giggles stopped behind her.

The casting director thought a moment and then said, "You are in love with a very special young man. It took you a long time to find each other, and you are very happy together. But now something urgent has come up, and you must go away. You must find the right way to break the news to him."

Taffy stared at Channing Crandall for an instant, thinking how close he was to describing her own life. She closed her eyes, and when she opened them again, Cory Dillon was standing beside her. Only this was an old-fashioned Cory, wearing a powdered wig and dressed in knee-length breeches. He was smiling and motioning for her to walk into a garden with him.

Taffy smoothed her long hoop skirt and said, "There's something important that I must tell you."

They walked along in silence for a moment as she tried to find the words. Finally she stopped and sat down beneath a tree, looking into his handsome face as he knelt beside her.

"I must go away soon. Tomorrow, as a matter of fact." She held up her hand to prevent him from interrupting. "It is because of a letter I received, containing proof that I am not who you think I am. According to the letter, my parents were traveling actors who stopped here one cold winter night and left me in the care of the people I've always called my parents. They left me here because I was frail, and they were afraid I could not survive the hardships of traveling from town to town. Now they are dying, and I must go to them before it is too late."

Tears streamed down Cory's face as he begged her to stay. Taffy fought back her own tears as she got to her feet.

"I must go, but I will always love you. And if there is a way for me to come back to you, I will. I promise with all my heart." Kissing the tip of a finger, she brushed it across his cheek, then turned and fled down the path.

There was not a sound in the room as Taffy pulled herself back to reality. Fear shot through her. Had she been that bad? Glancing quickly around, she saw to her amazement that there was hardly a dry eye in the class. Suddenly applause thundered from everywhere.

"Oh, Taffy. That was wonderful!" shrieked Mrs. Sinclair, rushing forward and smothering her with a gigantic hug.

Taffy turned. Channing Crandell was beaming at her.

"That was wonderful, Taffy, and it should prove to everyone here why you, and only you, will play Tiffany Stafford if the movie becomes a series," he said in an authoritative voice.

Taffy nodded and went back to her seat. She didn't

look at Summer or Cynthia. She didn't have to. She had ended any chance either of them had to take her role away from her—and she had done it by improvising saying good-bye to Cory.

"But can I do the scene as well if I have to say good-bye for real?" she whispered.

11❋

*M*onday was Clash Day, and Taffy went through her closet looking for the worst possible combination she could find. As she held up one piece of clothing after another in front of the mirror, she couldn't help remembering that it had been exactly one month ago— on Pajama Day—that she had returned from Hollywood to Wakeman Junior High. She winced as she remembered how awful it had been to be practically the only girl in school wearing regular clothes.

"I stuck out like a sore thumb," she told her reflection. "But not today."

A lot had happened in that month, she thought. She still missed Hollywood as much as she had at first, but at least she was starting to feel like she belonged at Wacko. Still, that could all change again if *Nobody Likes Tiffany Stafford* becomes a television series, she reminded herself.

Taffy finally settled on a bright orange pullover sweater that she seldom wore because it made her complexion look a sick shade of green. Next she put on a fuchsia miniskirt, and completed the outfit with flame red tights and black high-top shoes.

"That ought to do it," she giggled, dabbing on pink lipstick.

She was humming to herself as she gathered her books and jacket and hurried down to breakfast. Mr. Sinclair had already left for work, but her mother was sitting at the table sipping coffee and working the crossword puzzle in the morning newspaper.

"Morning, Mother," said Taffy.

"Morning, dear," replied Mrs. Sinclair. Then she glanced up. Her mouth dropped open, her eyes got enormous, and she nearly dropped her coffee cup. "Taffy! What's wrong with you? And why are you wearing that outfit? You look *ghastly*!"

Taffy twirled around to give her mother the full effect of her outrageous clothes. Then she laughed and said, "Don't worry. Today is Clash Day. Everybody will be dressed like this."

"I don't care if it's Insanity Day, you're not leaving the house like that!" her mother stormed. "What if someone *saw* you in that get-up? Someone *important?*"

"If you mean Channing Crandall, I'm sure he's gone back to Hollywood by now," Taffy assured her. "Like I said, everybody at school will be wearing horrible outfits. I'll just blend into the scenery."

"Taffy, I'm serious," warned her mother. "You are not leaving this house dressed that way. Now, go upstairs immediately and change into something presentable."

"You don't understand! I have to wear this. It's important! I want to be like everybody else."

"You are not like everybody else, dear. You are special."

"Mo-*ther!*" Taffy cried.

Mrs. Sinclair rose from her chair like an erupting volcano. "*Taffy!*" she roared. "Did you hear me?"

Tears spilled from Taffy's eyes. She dropped her books on the table with a thud and stomped back upstairs. Why does she always have to be so paranoid? Taffy sobbed to herself as she flung open her closet door and stared at the row of perfectly matched outfits inside. But there was no use arguing. Her mother always got her way. Always!

❖ ❖ ❖

When Taffy neared school a little later, she debated leaving her jacket on, thinking maybe kids wouldn't notice that the white denim skirt and the red-and-white knit top she wore under the jacket looked great together.

"Hey, Taffy. Let's see what you're wearing," Shawnie called from behind her.

Taffy turned around to see her friend racing up the sidewalk in a wacky combination of brightly colored prints and stripes.

"Isn't this fun?" Shawnie asked breathlessly. Then she stopped and looked at Taffy in disbelief. "Hey, today's Clash Day. Don't you want to fit in?"

Taffy fought to keep Shawnie from seeing the tears of embarrassment forming behind her eyes as she told Shawnie about the scene with her mother.

"Gosh, I'm sorry," murmured Shawnie, and the girls walked the rest of the way to school in silence.

All day long Taffy felt out of place. All the other kids seemed to be having a ball in their crazy outfits, and she was sure some of them were whispering about her as she went from class to class. They probably think I'm too conceited to wear anything that clashes, she thought. Shawnie's words played over and over in her mind. *Don't you want to fit in?* Of course I do, she thought miserably, but how can I?

❧   ❧   ❧

When Taffy got home from school that afternoon, she found another letter with a Hollywood postmark. But this one wasn't from Paige. Taffy sucked in her breath and stared at the return address. It was from Raven! She snatched it from the stack of letters in the mailbox and hurried to her room before her mother could spot it and demand to know what it said.

Dear Taffy,
I'm sorry I haven't written sooner. I got your address from Paige a long time ago and started about a dozen letters to you, but I tore them all up. The trouble was, none of them sounded quite right. I guess what I really want to say is that I miss you a lot and want you to come back to Hollywood. I was sincere when I said I'd like to take you out.
We should be hearing soon about the TV series. We're all crossing our fingers.
Well, that's all for now. Write soon, and don't forget your friends in Hollywood!

Love,
Raven

Taffy read the letter at least a hundred times. Then she stretched out on her bed and closed her eyes. She could see the palm trees swaying on the boulevards in Hollywood and hear the waves lapping against the shore at Venice Beach. She could see Paige Kramer's bright red hair and flashing smile, and tiny Tess, who looked six or seven but was really fifteen. Paige and Tess were terrific friends, and so was KJ, who was always wise-cracking and making jokes on the set. But most of all she could see gorgeous Raven Blaine, smiling at her, saying that he wanted to take her out.

She sighed, thinking about how much she missed Raven and all her Hollywood friends, and how she missed studying her lines and being in front of the cameras. She missed being a *professional*! She giggled to herself, remembering the Media Club's set and the tiny camcorder Jon Smith had used to film the program. There was nothing professional about that.

I could never stand being a member of Media Club, even for Shawnie, she admitted to herself. How could I ever have thought I belonged there? How could I ever have believed I belong at Wakeman Junior High, where everyone is jealous of me and whispers behind my back? No! The truth is, I want to go back to Hollywood. That's where I really fit in.

Taffy had trouble sleeping that night. There was no doubt now. She had made up her mind. If the movie became a television series, she would return to Hollywood. It was the only choice, now that she thought about it. She would never fit in at Wakeman Junior High, no matter how hard she tried.

But what about Cory? she thought. How can I possibly keep going steady with him if I go back to Hollywood? And what if Raven asks me out? I can't go, she told herself sadly. But I can't break up with Cory, either. He'll be so hurt.

And what about Shawnie? she asked herself. She's my best friend. How can I just desert her? Of course, she does have Kimm, Taffy reasoned. A tiny flame of jealousy flared at the thought of Kimm. First she tries to steal my best friend, and now she's after my boy-friend. How can I just go off and let Kimm get away with that?

Taffy flopped over onto her stomach and buried her face in her pillow. I'll just have to face it when and *if* the time comes, she decided.

12✻

*T*affy waited until dinner was over and her parents were settled in the family room, watching a news program on TV. Then she excused herself and went quietly to the phone in the upstairs hall to call Shawnie without being overheard. She was bursting to tell someone about her letter from Raven, and Shawnie was the only one she could tell.

The phone had scarcely rung once when Shawnie's mother answered.

"Hi, Mrs. Pendergast, this is Taffy Sinclair. May I please speak to Shawnie?"

"I'm sorry, Taffy, but Shawnie is doing her homework. You'll have to speak to her at school in the morning," Mrs. Pendergast said curtly.

Taffy sighed. She had forgotten how strict Shawnie's parents were. They controlled her time and her activities more than any other parents Taffy could think of. "Thanks," she murmured dejectedly and hung up.

Taffy tried to begin her own homework, but her eyes kept being drawn like twin magnets to the letter from Raven lying on the edge of her desk.

"He wasn't kidding when he said he liked me the night before I left Hollywood," she whispered to herself. "He does! *He does! HE DOES!*"

But what about Cory? asked a little voice in her mind.

Taffy sat up straight and frowned. "What about him?" she answered angrily. "Nobody even knows yet if I'm staying here or going back to Hollywood."

Just the same, she knew she couldn't say a word about Raven to anyone who might tell Cory.

The next morning Taffy motioned wildly to Shawnie the instant she saw her across the school grounds. "Hurry! I've got something to show you," she called.

Shawnie's eyes were glowing with excitement when she reached Taffy. "What is it? Did you hear some news about the TV series?"

Taffy shook her head and grinned. "Better than that," she said. "Guess."

"I can't. Oh, Taffy, don't keep me in suspense," begged Shawnie. "What is it?"

Taffy reached into her jacket pocket and pulled out Raven's letter with a dramatic flourish. "Feast your eyes," she commanded.

Shawnie's mouth dropped open as she clutched the envelope and read the return address. "Oh, my gosh!" she shrieked at the top of her lungs. "It's a letter from Raven Blaine!"

"Shh!" said Taffy, but it was too late. All around them, kids stopped their own conversations to stare at Taffy and Shawnie.

"Oh, no," Taffy wailed. "I wanted to keep it a secret. Now everybody knows."

Shawnie looked mortified. "I'm sorry, Taffy," she said. "I didn't mean to. It's just that . . . well . . . I mean, a letter from Raven Blaine! I guess I just went berserk!"

Taffy glanced around quickly. No one was looking at them anymore. Maybe, just maybe, no one had heard Shawnie.

"I tried to call you last night to tell you," said Taffy, "but your mother wouldn't let me talk to you."

Shawnie rolled her eyes. "It figures," she said, and began reading the letter. "Wow. He says he missed you and wants you to come back to Hollywood. Gosh, Taffy. Raven Blaine—*the* Raven Blaine—wants to go out with you! How can you stand it? It's the most exciting thing I've ever heard of! How can you even *breathe*?"

"I keep pinching myself to be sure I'm awake," Taffy

admitted. "But you know what bothers me . . . Cory. Oh, Shawnie, I like him, too. Honest. I really do."

Shawnie gave Taffy a sympathetic sigh. "Yeah, and so does Kimm. I've been watching how she looks at him. What are you going to do?"

"I don't know," said Taffy. "But I'm sure not going to break up with Cory and let Kimm have him. That much I know."

❁   ❁   ❁

Taffy was in third-period English class later that morning when a student messenger from the office entered the classroom and handed Miss Dickinson a note. The teacher read the note quickly and then said, "Taffy, Mr. Bell would like to see you in his office right away. You may take your books in case you're not back before the bell."

Taffy nodded and murmured thank you to Miss Dickinson. As she hurried down the hallway, she tried to figure out what Mr. Bell could want.

I couldn't be in trouble, she reasoned. I haven't done anything. Yikes. I hope nothing is wrong at home.

When she got to the office, Mr. Bell motioned her to his desk, all smiles. "Come on in, Taffy. I have some good news, and I wanted you to hear it before I announce it to the school over the public address system."

Taffy blinked at the principal. Things were getting more mysterious by the minute.

"Your mother just called," Mr. Bell went on, "and

Nobody Likes Tiffany Stafford is going to be shown on television at four P.M. tomorrow. Isn't that wonderful news?"

Taffy nodded eagerly. "Tomorrow?" she murmured. "I didn't expect it to be shown quite so soon." Then something else Mr. Bell had said caught her attention. "You're going to announce it to the whole school?"

"Of course," Mr. Bell assured her. "I'm sure everyone will want to watch. It's not every day our school can boast it has its own movie star."

Taffy couldn't suppress a smile. Now everyone would see what a good actress she was. Let's see how they treat me after that, she thought smugly.

Mr. Bell made the announcement during the next period, and for the rest of the day the school buzzed with excitement. Kids even stopped Taffy in the halls to ask her about the movie.

"They act as if they don't really believe it," she complained to Shawnie after school.

"It's like I told you before," said Shawnie. "Nobody from Wacko has ever done anything like it, so it's hard for some kids to imagine."

"Why don't you come over to my house tomorrow and watch the movie with me," suggested Taffy. "We could even make it into a party and invite Cory and Craig."

"Wow. That would be terrific," replied Shawnie. "I'll talk to Craig if you want me to."

"Okay," said Taffy. "I'll ask Cory."

Taffy waited at Cory's locker after school. She had thought up the party on the spur of the moment, and now she was a little nervous. What if her friends didn't think her acting was great after all?

Of course it's great, she told herself sternly. But down deep she knew that that wasn't what was really bothering her. What would Cory think when he saw her on the screen with Raven? Maybe she shouldn't have suggested a party. Maybe she should have planned to watch in private.

But it was too late to change her mind, and when she told Cory about the party, his face lit up. "Sure," he said. "It sounds great. I can't believe you're really going to be in front of us on the screen." Then his face clouded, and he added, "This doesn't mean you're going back to Hollywood, does it?"

It was the question Taffy had been dreading. She took a deep breath and crossed her fingers behind her back before she answered. "Of course not. The producers haven't made any decisions about the TV series yet. As far as I know, I'll be at Wacko forever."

13*

*T*affy hurried home the next day after school to make sure everything was ready. Her father had left work early and was in the family room, setting up the VCR to tape the movie. Her mother bustled around in the kitchen, putting chips in a bowl and setting out cans of soda for Taffy and her friends.

"Oh, this is so exciting," gushed Mrs. Sinclair. "My own *baby* is a movie star."

"Mo-*ther*," said Taffy. "I'm not a baby."

Just then the doorbell rang, and Taffy rushed to answer.

"Hi, guys," she said to Shawnie, Cory, and Craig, who were clustered on the front step. "Come on in."

"Hey, it's only fifteen minutes till show time," said Cory. "Just think, millions of kids all across America

95

are going to be watching *you*!" He pointed at Taffy and grinned.

"Isn't that fantastic?" said Shawnie. "I can't believe this is really happening."

"Me, either," murmured Taffy, feeling suddenly nervous at the thought of so many teenagers sitting in front of their television sets at this very moment, getting ready to watch her acting debut. And what about Paige and Tess and Raven? Were they watching, too? She had a funny feeling at the back of her throat, as if she might throw up from excitement, and she swallowed hard to get rid of it.

"I've got refreshments for everyone," Mrs. Sinclair sang as she entered the family room carrying the bowl of chips in one hand and a tray of sodas in the other.

Taffy was too antsy to sit down. She watched her friends get settled around the room as if they were about to watch an ordinary show. Shawnie was on the sofa. Cory sank into a chair, and Craig sat on the floor between the sofa and chair.

Taffy checked her watch. Five minutes to go. Her palms were sweaty, and she wiped them on her jeans and looked at her friends. Craig and Cory were talking quietly, and Shawnie was munching chips.

How can they be so calm? she wondered. If I could just go to my room and hide until this is over . . . or maybe for the rest of my life if I give a rotten performance!

"It's time," her father announced. He waved the remote control unit toward the television, and the screen flashed to life.

"Look! There are the opening credits!" cried Mrs. Sinclair.

Taffy felt her knees turn to jelly as she sank onto the floor in front of the set. Every eye in the room was on the screen.

"Bouquets and Rainbows Productions presents . . ." Taffy murmured as she read the words on the screen. ". . . *Nobody Likes Tiffany Stafford* . . . starring Raven Blaine . . . Paige Kramer . . . Taffy Sinclair—"

"*Taffy Sinclair!*" shrieked Shawnie. "Did you see it? It said Taffy Sinclair, right *there*!"

Everyone was nodding and laughing as a stream of commercials came on next, and Shawnie collapsed across the sofa, her arms flung out wide. "I don't believe it," she moaned. "I knew it was going to happen, but I still don't believe it."

"Shh, everybody," said Cory. "It's starting."

The room grew quiet again. Taffy squinted at first, looking out nervously through narrow slits, but as the first scene faded in, she gradually relaxed and watched eagerly. It almost seemed as if she were back on the set. Paige Kramer looked like a true villain as she and her two best friends ganged up against Tiffany Stafford, the character Taffy played. Then Raven came on the scene, looking almost as handsome on screen as he did in person. The sight of Raven made Taffy blush, and she turned her head slightly so that Cory wouldn't see.

At the next commercial break, Cory turned to Taffy. "Hey, it's pretty obvious that your character has a thing for that guy," he said, putting extra emphasis on the word "thing."

"Yeah," said Craig, and Shawnie giggled.

This time Taffy could not hide her scarlet face. "It's just a movie," she argued. "I mean, I had to do what the script said."

"Who would argue about a thing like that?" asked Shawnie, rolling her eyes. "I'd have a crush on him even if it wasn't in the script."

"Do you mean to say that you didn't have a crush on Raven Blaine while you were in Hollywood?" asked Cory, and Taffy couldn't tell if he was joking or serious.

Eeeek, she thought. What do I say now?

She was still searching for the right answer when the doorbell rang.

"Don't anyone move. I'll get it," her mother called out as she hurried to open the door before the commercial ended and the movie resumed.

"Flowers for Miss Taffy Sinclair," said a man holding a long, white box.

Taffy looked at the box in surprise. "Who would be sending those?" she wondered softly.

"They must be from Jerry Lowenthal, your wonderful director," her mother said breathlessly.

Taffy took the box from her mother and opened it. Inside were a dozen beautiful long-stemmed red roses.

"There's a card!" shrieked Shawnie. "Hurry up, Taffy. Open it."

Taffy picked up the small white envelope while everyone looked on. Slipping the card out, she took a deep breath before reading the message.

For Taffy—the brightest star in Hollywood. Congratulations on a great performance. I miss you. Please come back soon.

> *Love,*
> *Raven*

Taffy's first instinct was to hide the card before Cory could see it, but when she glanced at him, she could tell by his expression that it was too late.

Taffy handed the roses to her mother, who bustled off into the kitchen to put them in water. She tried to think of something to say to Cory, but she couldn't. He had slumped back into his chair and was staring at the actors on the screen as if he weren't really seeing them. Shawnie and Craig were quiet, too.

Taffy turned her attention back to the television set. Here it is, she thought, my big debut. But somehow all the fun had gone out of it. She could hardly wait to see the words THE END flash across the screen.

14*

When Taffy got to school the next morning, she found Marge Whitworth, the anchorwoman for the local TV station, waiting on the front steps with her camera crew. Power cables crisscrossed the sidewalk to the station's van, parked nearby.

"Taffy!" called out Ms. Whitworth. "We'd like to interview you for the six-o'clock news."

"Sure," said Taffy. She put her books down on a step and whipped a brush and a small mirror out of her purse. "Just a minute while I fix my hair." An instant later she approached the anchorwoman and asked, "Do I look okay?"

"You look terrific," Marge Whitworth said.

A small crowd of students was beginning to gather.

Taffy could see Jana Morgan and Melanie Edwards among the faces. Taffy smiled to herself, remembering the last time she had been interviewed on TV by Marge Whitworth. It was last year, in sixth grade. She and Jana had found a baby girl named Ashley on the front steps of Mark Twain Elementary. That time Jana had been interviewed, too. But this time it was just Taffy in front of the camera.

I'm the star, she thought with satisfaction.

Marge Whitworth positioned Taffy on the steps and did a quick sound check. Then she signaled the cameraman and began the interview.

"Ladies and gentlemen, it's my pleasure to present to you our own local movie star, Taffy Sinclair, whose first movie, *Nobody Likes Tiffany Stafford*, was shown on network television last night. Taffy, can you tell us how it felt to see yourself on TV and to know that boys and girls all across America were watching, too?" asked Ms. Whitworth.

Taffy took a deep breath and looked straight into the camera. "It was a wonderful feeling," she said calmly. "I hope that everyone enjoyed watching the film as much as I enjoyed making it."

Taffy's heart swelled with pride when she heard a small ripple of applause somewhere in the crowd and saw out of the corner of her eye that it came from Shawnie and, surprisingly, from Kimm. Cory was standing with them, and Taffy saw with a stab of sadness that he wasn't applauding. He wasn't even smiling. He had left her house last night with barely a word, obviously angry about the roses.

Taffy was drawn back to the present by the sound of Marge Whitworth's voice. "Now, Taffy, can you tell us what was the most exciting part of making the movie?"

Taffy thought for a moment. "It's hard to pick out one thing as most exciting," she said. "I loved meeting the other stars, and working on the set, and, of course, going to Hollywood parties and to the beach."

Marge Whitworth asked several more questions before ending the interview. Then she thanked Taffy and moved back toward the van, where her crew was busy storing the equipment away.

Taffy watched her go, thinking that it felt good to be in front of a camera again. How could I ever give that up to go back to being an ordinary student? she wondered.

"Talk about a celebrity," called out Kimm as she and Shawnie rushed toward Taffy. "We're going to get to see you on television again tonight."

Taffy laughed. "Talk about overexposure," she said. "You guys are going to get sick of turning on your TVs and seeing my face."

"No, seriously," said Kimm, "I just loved watching your movie last night. You were terrific. You have every right to feel proud of yourself."

Taffy blinked in surprise. She hadn't expected so much flattery from Kimm.

"Thanks, Kimm," she said. "I heard you sing with Cory's band earlier this year, and you're pretty terrific, too."

Kimm smiled broadly. "Thanks, but that's nothing compared to being a movie star." Looking around quickly, she added, "Hey, I've got to run. I'll see you guys later."

Taffy watched Kimm hurry toward the building. "I have to admit that you were right about Kimm," she said to Shawnie. "She is nice."

"I knew you'd think so when you got to know her better," replied Shawnie.

"I do like her, except for one thing," said Taffy, frowning. "She has a crush on Cory."

"I'm not positive," said Shawnie. "Naturally they're together a lot because of all the rehearsals. It could just be my imagination. I guess I shouldn't have mentioned it, but . . ." Her voice trailed off as she gazed over Taffy's shoulder. "Uh-oh," she murmured.

Taffy whirled around, following Shawnie's gaze.

"Oh, no," she said. It was Cory whom Kimm had been rushing to see. They stood together near the front door, deep in conversation.

"What am I going to do now?" she cried. "He's mad because of the roses that Raven sent me. What if he decides he likes Kimm now instead of me?"

Shawnie looked serious for a moment. "There's something else I should probably tell you," she said. "He's been getting a lot of teasing about you lately."

Taffy flashed her a surprised look. "Teasing about me?" she echoed in astonishment.

"Right. In the hall between classes a couple of days

ago I overheard a bunch of guys asking him if you were going to use your influence in Hollywood to get his band into the big time. I could tell that it made him awfully mad."

"That's terrible," exclaimed Taffy. "Those creeps! Why would they say a thing like that?"

"I guess everybody thinks of you differently now. You're our resident celebrity, and they don't know how to handle it," Shawnie offered sadly.

The bell rang, and the girls said good-bye and headed for their lockers. Taffy felt more confused than ever. Now even Cory was having trouble because she was a movie star.

I'd better keep my fingers crossed that the movie does become a series, she thought, because I'm never going to fit in again at Wakeman.

❁   ❁   ❁

Taffy was still thinking about her predicament when she and Shawnie headed out of the building after school. Suddenly Shawnie stopped and pointed toward the street.

"Look, Taffy!" she cried excitedly. "There's a limousine at the curb, and your mother's standing beside it."

Taffy looked up quickly. A long, white limousine was parked between two yellow school buses, and standing beside it, just as Shawnie had said, was Mrs. Sinclair, waving frantically in Taffy's direction.

"Oh, my gosh," Taffy murmured.

"Taffy! Guess what?" shouted her mother. "Channing Crandall is back in town. He sent this limo to get you and take you to The Merry Chase Acting Studio to see him. Oh, Taffy. I know it can only mean one thing. Hurry, dear. We can't keep Mr. Crandall waiting."

Taffy nodded and turned to Shawnie, but she couldn't look at her right away. Her mother was probably right. There was only one thing this could mean. She was going back to Hollywood. But for herself and Shawnie it would mean saying good-bye again. How could she be so excited and so sad at the same time?

"I guess I'd better go," said Taffy.

Shawnie nodded and cleared her throat. "Right," she said softly. "And, Taffy . . . good luck."

Taffy got into the backseat of the limousine and pretended to stare out the window so that her mother couldn't see the tears streaming down her face.

❂   ❂   ❂

"Well, if it isn't the brightest new star in Hollywod," said Channing Crandall when Taffy and her mother stepped into the studio. He strode forward, grinning broadly, and clasped her small hand in his large one. Merry Chase was beaming beside him.

"Congratulations, love," she said in her deep, throaty voice.

"The ratings are in from last night's broadcast of *Nobody Likes Tiffany Stafford*," Mr. Crandall went on, "and I'm pleased to tell you that they were spectacular. That's all the producers were waiting for. Good ratings mean that we're going to turn the movie into a series, *and . . .*" The casting director paused to build suspense. "And we'd like to have the same cast, which means that you have the starring role of Tiffany Stafford again if you want it. What do you say? Will you do it?"

Taffy couldn't answer right away, although she could see her mother twisting her hands nervously.

"We have the first three scripts completed already, so we'd like to start filming next week," the casting director added.

Taffy stared at Channing Crandall. This was it. If she said yes, her life would change forever. She would have to leave Wakeman Junior High for six long months. She would have to leave her best friend and her steady boyfriend. She would never be a normal teenager again.

She closed her eyes. No, she thought as a smile spread slowly across her face. I'll never be normal again, but I'll be a *star.*

15✿

"**N**othing's definite yet," Taffy said when Shawnie called her later in the evening after the interview with Marge Whitworth had been broadcast. She knew she was lying to her best friend, but she still didn't know how to break the news.

"When will you know?" Shawnie asked.

"Pretty soon," replied Taffy, wondering if her voice was giving her away. "If I do go back to Hollywood," she added slowly, "you'll have Kimm to be friends with, won't you?"

There was a long pause. "Sure," said Shawnie, "but believe me, it won't be the same."

Taffy bit her lip to keep from crying. *It won't be the same for me, either,* she wanted to say. Instead she went on, "But you were telling me how much fun it is to go to her house, and how interesting she is."

"Yeah, I know," said Shawnie, sounding more and more dejected, "and I meant it, but. . . . Let's change the subject, okay?"

After they hung up, Taffy stared at the phone for a while. Finally she looked up Kimm's number and dialed it.

"Hi, Kimm," she said when the girl answered. "This is Taffy. Can you talk a minute?"

"Sure," Kimm replied. "I watched your interview on TV a few minutes ago, and it was great. What's up?"

Taffy chose her words carefully. "When I first got home from Hollywood, I was pretty jealous of how much time you and Shawnie had spent together while I was gone."

"I know you guys are best friends," Kimm interjected. "I wasn't trying to wreck your friendship. Honest."

"I understand that now," said Taffy. "And it's okay that you and Shawnie like each other so much." She paused, not wanting to say what was coming next. "There's something else."

"What?" asked Kimm.

"Can you keep a secret?"

"Well . . . sure," said Kimm.

Taffy took a deep breath. "I found out after school today that *Nobody Likes Tiffany Stafford* is definitely going to become a television series and that I've got the starring role again."

"So you'll be going back to Hollywood?" asked Kimm.

"Right. Shawnie doesn't know yet. I didn't want to tell her until . . ."

"Oh, I get it. Until you knew she'd have a good friend while you're gone?" asked Kimm in a soft voice.

Taffy tried to say yes, but the word stuck in her throat. She waited a moment until the awful feeling had passed and then whispered, "That's right. I leave on Sunday."

"Don't worry," said Kimm. "Shawnie and I will be good friends while you're gone. Not only that, we'll both be your friends when you come home."

❃ ❃ ❃

Taffy couldn't keep her secret much longer. Her mother was telling everyone she knew. She even called the local newspaper.

"When are you going to be leaving?" Shawnie asked sadly. They were sitting on the front steps of the school after lunch the next day.

"Sunday," said Taffy. "Mother's checking with the airlines today." She paused a moment. "I just want you to know that as much as I want to do the series, it makes me sad to leave. I wish there was some way you could come with me."

"Maybe I can come and visit you during summer vacation," offered Shawnie.

"Do you think you could?" Taffy asked excitedly. "Would your parents let you?"

"I'll do anything to talk them into it if you'll promise me one thing," said Shawnie.

Taffy looked at her in surprise. "What's that?"

Shawnie glanced up to make sure no one was listening. Then she giggled and whispered, "Introduce me to Raven Blaine!"

Taffy laughed, too, and for a moment the whole idea of going back to her movie career seemed exciting again. Then she thought of Cory.

"I'll introduce you to Raven anytime, especially if you can help me figure out what to do about Cory. I can't go steady with him if I'm going to be gone for such a long time," she said, looking pleadingly at Shawnie. "But how can I break up with him without hurting him or making him think I'm stuck-up and conceited? No matter what I say, that's how it's going to sound."

Shawnie squeezed Taffy's hand. "I don't know," she admitted. "I guess all you can do is try. There he is, over by the bike rack. Why don't you talk to him now, before he hears about it from someone else?"

Taffy glanced toward Cory. He was standing alone, wearing the same sad expression he'd had ever since Raven's roses had arrived. He knows, she thought. But Shawnie's right. I have to talk to him now.

"Hi, Cory," she called out as she approached the bike rack. "Do you have a minute?"

"Sure," he said. A smile flickered across his face and then died away. "How's it going?"

"Okay." She paused, fighting to keep her nerve. "I have something to tell you."

Cory ran a finger across the top of the bike rack. Without looking at her, he said, "You're going back to Hollywood, right?"

Tears filled Taffy's eyes. She tried to say yes, but all she could do was nod. Finally she cleared her throat and said, "Part of me wants to stay here with you and Shawnie. The trouble is, I don't fit in anymore. Nobody likes me. Everyone thinks I'm conceited."

"Is that the only reason you want to go back?" asked Cory.

Cory's words startled Taffy. It was the one question she didn't want to answer, but she knew she had to. "No," she admitted. "I really do want to be a star."

"And singing with The Dreadful Alternatives would never make you a star, at least not a big star," said Cory.

Taffy started to protest, but Cory shook his head. "It's true. You're special. You belong in Hollywood." He paused and said softly, "I guess I shouldn't even get mad if you go out with Raven Blaine."

"But . . . Cory . . ." Taffy sputtered.

"It's okay. I've been thinking about it a lot since he sent you those roses. I won't get mad if you go out with Raven Blaine. But I don't want you to get mad, either, if I go out with Kimm."

Taffy stared at him in astonishment. She didn't know what to say.

"See, it's not that I don't like you as much as ever," Cory continued. "I do. No one can take your place. Honest. But Kimm's nice. And we have lots of fun together . . . the same way you have fun with your friends in Hollywood."

Taffy wanted to hug Cory, right there on the school grounds with half the student body watching. He did understand, after all. It was too wonderful to be true.

Instead she smiled shyly and said, "Thanks, Cory. I'm leaving Sunday, but I'll be back."

"Yeah," he said. "In six months. That'll be great."

When the bell rang a few minutes later, Taffy headed for her afternoon classes feeling better than she had in a long time. She could leave for Hollywood now knowing that everything was settled with Shawnie and Cory, partly—she smiled and shook her head in disbelief—because of Kimm, the girl she had thought of as an enemy just a few days before.

❁   ❁   ❁

On Friday after school Cory stopped her in the hall.

"I know that you're leaving on Sunday, and that you'll be busy packing, but I'd really like you to come to The Dreadful Alternatives rehearsal tomorrow afternoon. Do you think you could talk your mom into letting you stop by?"

"Wow," said Taffy. "You want me to come to a rehearsal even though we've broken up."

Cory grinned. "Sure. Why not? Anyway, do you think your mom will let you?"

Taffy sighed. "I don't know. You know how she is."

"Will you try?" asked Cory. "It's important to me that you be there."

Taffy took a deep breath and let it out slowly. Why did he want her to come to rehearsal now that she was leaving town? she wondered. They had already agreed that she'd never get to sing with his band. But maybe it would be all right to go. After all, he still liked her, and she still liked him.

"Okay," she said. "I'll talk to her."

✿ ✿ ✿

Mrs. Sinclair was impossible to convince.

"Taffy, you know that we have a lot to do before our flight on Sunday. How can you possibly ask to go to some band rehearsal?"

"It's not just *some* band rehearsal," Taffy argued. "It's Cory's band, and he wants me to be there. It will be six months before I'll see him again. Please let me go. *Pleeease*. I'll get everything done. I promise."

"Absolutely not," said her mother in the tone of voice that told Taffy it was useless to argue.

She trudged up to her room and closed the door. What am I going to do now? she wondered as she took a sweater out of a drawer, folded it, and placed it in her suitcase. I really want to go to that rehearsal!

A little later she heard the phone ring. She listened at the door for a moment, hoping it was for her, but her mother didn't call her. Resignedly she went back to her packing. After a few minutes there was a soft knock on her bedroom door.

"Who is it?" Taffy called.

"It's your mother, dear. May I come in?"

"Sure," she replied.

Mrs. Sinclair came into the room and sat down in the chair beside Taffy's desk. "I've been thinking," she said slowly, and then paused.

Taffy waited, but when her mother didn't say anything else, she frowned and asked, "Thinking about what?"

Her mother gave Taffy a brief smile. "Well, depending on how your packing is coming along, of course, maybe it would be all right for you to go to the band rehearsal tomorrow."

Taffy's mouth dropped open. "Do you mean that?" she cried. When her mother nodded, Taffy began jumping up and down. "Oh, thank you! Thank you! I'll get all my packing finished ahead of time. I promise."

❁   ❁   ❁

When Taffy arrived at Cory's house the next afternoon, she parked her bike and walked slowly up the front steps of the two-story Colonial house, hesitating a moment before knocking. Cory opened the door.

"Hi, Taffy. Come on in," he said.

Taffy followed Cory inside, thinking he seemed strangely uneasy. She glanced around the silent living room. "Where is everybody?"

"Oh . . . well, they're downstairs in the family room getting set up," he replied.

He took her jacket, but he didn't head for the stairs.

"Aren't we going down, too?" she asked. "They can't rehearse without you."

Cory blinked at her and looked at his watch. "Oh, sure," he said. Then he moved toward the stairway and said in an unusually loud voice, "Sure, Taffy. Let's go on downstairs."

Taffy raised an eyebrow and gave him a puzzled look. Then she went down the stairs behind him.

"SURPRISE!" came a chorus of voices as kids jumped out from behind sofas and chairs, giggling and squealing. "SURPRISE! SURPRISE!"

At first Taffy could only stand in the middle of the room, staring at the dozens of boys and girls swarming around her. Alexis Duvall and Lisa Snow had big smiles on their faces. Mona Vaughn looked as if she might explode with joy, and from every direction kids were calling her name and grinning. Even The Fabulous Five were there. Balloons floated overhead, and at one end of the room stood a table covered with refreshments.

Suddenly Shawnie rushed up and gave Taffy a hug. "We all got together to say good-bye."

"And, brother, did we have a tough time getting you here," smiled Kimm. "Shawnie had to call your mother and beg her to let you come."

"But . . ." Taffy fumbled. "All these kids . . . I thought . . ."

"You thought nobody likes you," Shawnie said

softly, "but you were wrong. They may not be your *best* friends, and they may get jealous of you sometimes. But you're still a Wacko kid, and everyone admires your talent."

"Most of them just had to get used to the idea of having a movie star for a classmate," interjected Kimm. "But they're starting to understand better now."

"Yeah," said Cory. "They don't think you're stuck-up. They know that you're special, that you belong in Hollywood, just as the rest of us belong here at Wacko."

Taffy felt her eyes fill with tears. She would never have dreamed that a moment like this could happen.

"Yeah, Taffy!"

"Congratulations!"

The air was filled with happy chatter as one after another of Taffy's classmates came forward to wish her success with the new series.

"How soon will it be on TV?" asked Randy Kirwan, who was there with Jana Morgan.

"I don't know," replied Taffy, "but we're going to start shooting on Monday."

"Maybe you could get Igor a part in one of the episodes," said Shane Arrington, referring to his pet iguana. "He's a big ham, and he's wanted to get into show business for ages."

"I'll see what I can do," Taffy promised, laughing.

It was then that she noticed Beth Barry standing a

little to the side. Am I imagining it, or does she look like she wants to talk to me? thought Taffy.

Taffy approached her, and Beth flashed a big smile. "I have to admit that I wish I were in your shoes," Beth said. "Any tips for an aspiring *amateur* actress?"

Taffy returned Beth's smile and rolled her eyes. "Get out of the Media Club," she said, groaning. "After that, you might see if you can get into one of Merry Chase's acting classes."

"Thanks," said Beth. "And, Taffy . . ." she added. "Good luck in Hollywood."

"Right," echoed Katie Shannon and Melanie Edwards, who had just walked up.

Taffy felt her throat tighten. Even her old enemies, The Fabulous Five, were wishing her luck. She couldn't let anyone see the tears that were threatening to spill from her eyes, so she nodded her thanks and turned around quickly, shouting to the others. "Hey, I *thought* this was going to be a band rehearsal for The Dreadful Alternatives. Why don't you guys play something?"

A cheer went up, and Cory and the other members of the band scrambled to tune their instruments, while Kimm took her place in front, ready to sing. Taffy watched her talk to Cory for a moment. They do look right together, she realized.

Taffy couldn't remember when she had had such a great time. She danced till her feet ached, stuffed herself with brownies and punch, and by the time the afternoon was almost over and most of the kids had gone home, she knew she was truly going to miss Wakeman Junior High.

"Cory, this is the most wonderful party I've ever had," she said, gesturing around at the empty soda cans and half-eaten cookies that now littered the room.

"I'm glad you liked it," he said. He lowered his eyes and drew her to him, kissing her softly on the lips. "That's for good-bye and this is for good luck," he said, kissing her again.

When Taffy rode her bike home, she felt as if she were floating on clouds. She couldn't believe how well everything had turned out. Maybe she didn't exactly fit in at Wakeman Junior High anymore, but at least she had learned that a lot of kids cared about her and wished her the best.

She smiled and whispered, "No Hollywood movie could ever have a happier ending."

If you liked this book, you'll love the previous Taffy Sinclair books by Betsy Haynes. That's where Jana Morgan, Katie Shannon, Christie Winchell, Melanie Edwards, and Beth Barry form a club called The Fabulous Five in order to keep up with the snootiest (and prettiest) girl in their class—Taffy! In these funny stories, Taffy stops at nothing to outdo Jana and the rest of The Fabulous Five. She tries blackmail, starring in a TV soap opera, and even being friendly, but together The Fabulous Five manage to stay one step ahead of their archenemy, the perfectly gorgeous, perfectly awful Taffy Sinclair!

You can follow Taffy and The Fabulous Five's fifth- and sixth-grade adventures and find out how it all started in these Taffy Sinclair books available from Bantam Skylark Books:

THE AGAINST TAFFY SINCLAIR CLUB

It was bad enough when Taffy Sinclair was just a pretty face. But now that's she developing faster than Jana Morgan and her four best friends, it's all-out war! What Jana and her friends don't know is that even the best-laid plans can backfire suddenly.

TAFFY SINCLAIR STRIKES AGAIN

It's time gorgeous Taffy Sinclair had a little competition. That's why Jana Morgan and her friends form The Fabulous Five, a self-improvement club. But when the third club meeting ends in disaster, Jana finds she has four new enemies. And with enemies like these, there's only one friend worth having . . . Taffy Sinclair!

TAFFY SINCLAIR, QUEEN OF THE SOAPS

Taffy Sinclair has done it again! This time, she's landed a role in a soap opera, playing a beautiful girl on her deathbed. Is there any way at all for The Fabulous Five to fight back against Taffy Sinclair, the TV star?

TAFFY SINCLAIR AND THE
ROMANCE MACHINE DISASTER

Taffy Sinclair is furious when she finds out that Jana Morgan is the first girl at Mark Twain Elementary to have a date with Randy Kirwan. Taffy gets her revenge when their sixth-grade teacher conducts a computer matchup game and nine other girls besides Jana turn out to be a "perfect match" with Randy!

BLACKMAILED BY TAFFY SINCLAIR

Taffy Sinclair has never been *this* terrible! When Jana finds a wallet that turns out to be stolen property, and Taffy catches her with it, Taffy makes Jana her personal slave. Jana is stuck serving Taffy her lunch, carrying her books, and worst of all, being her friend, until the rest of The Fabulous Five can help prove her innocence.

TAFFY SINCLAIR, BABY ASHLEY, AND ME

Jana and Taffy are on their way to the principal's office after having an argument in class when they find an abandoned baby on the front steps of the school. The two girls rescue baby Ashley, and become overnight celebrities. But can two archenemies share the limelight?

TAFFY SINCLAIR AND THE
SECRET ADMIRER EPIDEMIC

Jana Morgan has been receiving love notes from a secret admirer! And when Taffy Sinclair finds out, she's sure to be jealous. The Fabulous Five set out to uncover the identity of Jana's secret admirer . . . and uncover a big surprise instead.

TAFFY SINCLAIR AND THE
MELANIE MAKE-OVER

When Taffy Sinclair tells Melanie about a new modeling school, Melanie talks The Fabulous Five into signing up. Soon Melanie is spending lots of time with Taffy Sinclair, who's promised to get Melanie professional modeling jobs. The Fabulous Five know Taffy's up to something. . . . Can they win Melanie back when Taffy's holding out the lure of a glamorous modeling career?

THE TRUTH ABOUT TAFFY SINCLAIR

Taffy finally gets her chance to tell the story of the rivalry between her and The Fabulous Five. It's the last week of sixth grade at Mark Twain Elementary School, and all the students are cleaning out their lockers. When some of the boys switch around everyone's belongings, most of the kids think the prank is funny. For Taffy Sinclair, however, it's no laughing matter. Her personal diary is missing, and now the whole school will learn the truth about Taffy Sinclair!

TAFFY SINCLAIR GOES TO HOLLYWOOD

Taffy Sinclair has landed the starring role in a TV movie called *Nobody Likes Tiffany Stafford*. It's the story of a beautiful girl whose life at school is made miserable by three best friends who despise her—a part that Taffy can really relate to. In fact, it sounds just like a script from her own experiences with The Fabulous Five! But Paige Kramer, another actress in the movie, thinks *she* should have been the star. Can Taffy stop Paige from stealing the part, or will she lose her chance for stardom—and to play love scenes opposite Raven Blaine, the handsomest teenage movie idol in Hollywood?

And don't forget about The Fabulous Five series by Betsy Haynes! In these books, The Fabulous Five are in junior high, where they still compete with Taffy, but also find themselves with a whole new group of friends—and enemies!

Follow their seventh-grade adventures in these books (and many more!) available from Bantam Skylark Books:

The Fabulous Five #1:

SEVENTH-GRADE RUMORS

On the first day of junior high school, The Fabulous Five meet a group of girls who call themselves The Fantastic Foursome and become instant archrivals. But soon Jana finds herself really liking one of the members of the group, and the rest of The Fabulous Five think she's a traitor.

The Fabulous Five #2:

THE TROUBLE WITH FLIRTING

When Melanie reads some flirting tips in a teen magazine, she can't resist testing them out on three different boys. The results are disastrous—and hilarious!

The Fabulous Five #3:

THE POPULARITY TRAP

The rest of The Fabulous Five talk Christie into running for president of the seventh grade, even though she doesn't want to be nominated. Can Christie find a way to do what she wants without disappointing her friends?

The Fabulous Five #4:
HER HONOR, KATIE SHANNON

Katie thinks it will be easy to be fair when she becomes a judge on Wakeman's new Teen Court. Then she develops a crush on one of the biggest troublemakers at school!

The Fabulous Five #5:
THE BRAGGING WAR

Beth's big mouth gets The Fabulous Five in trouble when she starts bragging about The Fabulous Five to The Fantastic Foursome. Her friends beg her to stop, but she can't resist making one more "little" boast!

The Fabulous Five #6
THE PARENT GAME

When Jana's Family Living class is assigned a project to act as parents for a week, she agrees to help Taffy Sinclair babysit her "children." Jana wants to help Taffy, but can her old archenemy actually be trusted?

The Fabulous Five #7:
THE KISSING DISASTER

When the other members of The Fabulous Five seem too busy to have time for her, Melanie starts trying to prove to them how popular she is. Disaster strikes when Melanie gets the "kissing disease," and no one at school will go near her!

The Fabulous Five #8:
THE RUNAWAY CRISIS

Katie's sense of fairness gets her into trouble when Shawnie Pendergast, a friend with parent problems, runs away—and wants to hide out in the Shannons' basement.

The Fabulous Five #9:
THE BOYFRIEND DILEMMA

Two boys are interested in dating Christie, but she's not interested in having a boyfriend yet. Can she prove to them—and everyone else at school—that a boy and girl can just be friends?

The Fabulous Five #10:
PLAYING THE PART

When Beth gets the lead role in the school play she's thrilled, but her boyfriend Keith isn't. It means Beth won't have time for anything else. Will she have to choose between stardom and romance?

And don't miss **Missing You,** *the newest Fabulous Five Super Edition, coming to your bookstore soon. In this story, The Fabulous Five learn to cope with Christie Winchell's move to London. Here are some scenes from* **Missing You:**

"You're the new girl from the States, aren't you?" asked the girl across the table. Christie remembered her from history class. She was small and had red hair. She looked a lot like Katie Shannon. But best of all, she was making conversation.

"Yes, I am. I'm Christie Winchell."

"I'm Eleanore Geach."

"Hi," responded Christie, glad for the first friendly gesture of the day.

"And I'm Phoebe Mahoney," said the girl from the bus who resembled Jana.

"I'm Nicki Smythe," said the girl who reminded Christie of Beth. Other girls introduced themselves. Christie had trouble catching all their names.

"Hi," said Christie, trying to include everyone.

She waited an instant, hoping one of them would say something else. When no one did, she went back to her food. She poked at it and wrinkled her nose as she tried to figure out what it was.

"Shepherd's pie," said Eleanore.

"What?" asked Christie.

"What's on your plate. It's shepherd's pie. It's beef and gravy with mashed potatoes on top. We have it lots."

"You remind me of one of my best friends back home," Christie told Eleanore.

"I do?"

"Yes. Her name's Katie Shannon, and you look a lot like her." She turned to Phoebe. "It's funny, but you look like one of my other very best friends, Jana Morgan. And you look like Beth Barry," she said to Nicki. "I've got another friend named Melanie Edwards back home. We call ourselves The Fabulous Five," she explained with pride.

"Sounds kind of airy-fairy to me," remarked Nicki. There was sarcasm in her voice. "It's for dead cert I'm not any Beth Barry or whatever her name is."

"Airy-fairy?"

Phoebe frowned at Nicki. "Never mind her. She's just being ratty. Mind your manners, Nicki, or I'll snitch on you."

Christie could hardly wait for lunch period to be over. Except for a few more words she and Eleanore exchanged and a few glances from Phoebe, Christie felt totally left out of the conversation at the table.

It was Nicki who dominated the table talk, and

the more Christie watched her, the more she felt she *was* a lot like Beth. All Nicki needed was to have on a wild outfit instead of a uniform. Her hair was already almost as spiky as Beth's.

It was easy to see that Phoebe, Eleanore, and Nicki were best friends. Watching them only made Christie more homesick.

Gradually the crowd in the dining room thinned, and Christie found herself sitting alone. She bit down hard on her lower lip as she felt tears welling up in her eyes. Getting up slowly, she picked up her tray and took it to the return. Even the woman collecting the dirty dishes didn't look at her. For the first time in her life, Christie felt as if she didn't exist.

Meanwhile, back at home . . .

Laura was headed for their booth, with Melissa, Tammy, and Funny right behind.

"Well, if it isn't The Fabulous Five minus one," said Laura. "I see you're still hanging together."

"You wish we wouldn't, don't you, Laura McCall?" retorted Beth. "We'll be friends long after your group has split up."

"Oh, is that so?" said Laura, gloating. "Alexis Duvall said you let her read Christie's latest letter. I heard she's already found another group of friends to take your place, and she's going to call *them* The Fabulous Five. It didn't take her long to replace you guys, did it?"

Melissa and Tammy were smiling and nodding

behind her. Funny looked as if she'd rather be some-place else.

"She has *not* replaced us!" Jana said emphatically. She was so angry that she bumped her soda, and it splashed on her shirt. "What do you expect her to do, act unfriendly to everyone in her new school?" she asked dabbing at her blouse with a napkin.

"Of course not, but that's different from replacing such totally awesome friends," Laura scoffed. "And from what I heard, she's found someone to replace all of you except Melanie. I guess the rest of you were probably easy, but she'll have a hard time finding someone as boy crazy as you, Melanie."

Melanie looked as if she were going to explode. But before she could say anything, Laura twirled, whipping her long braid behind her shoulder.

The Fabulous Five stared after her. Their eyes were shooting fire.

"Christie's wanting to have friends just like us is a compliment," said Katie sticking out her chin defiantly. "We're special to her. So why *wouldn't* she want to hang around other people like us?"

"That's right," agreed Beth. "That just proves how much we mean to her. . . ."

ABOUT THE AUTHOR

BETSY HAYNES, the daughter of a former news-woman, began scribbling poetry and short stories as soon as she learned to write. A serious writing career, however, had to wait until after her marriage and the arrival of her two children. But that early practice must have paid off, for within three months Mrs. Haynes had sold her first story. In addition to a number of magazine short stories, The Fabulous Five and Taffy Sinclair series, Mrs. Haynes is also the author of *The Great Mom Swap* and its sequel, *The Great Boyfriend Trap.* She lives in Marco Island, Florida, with her husband, who is also an author.

THE FABULOUS FIVE

SUPER EDITION- SUPER OFFER!

SEND IN FOR YOUR CHANCE TO RECEIVE A FREE SPECIALLY AUTOGRAPHED LIMITED EDITION OF THE FABULOUS FIVE SUPER EDITION: *MISSING YOU*.

If you love Betsy Haynes' books about Taffy Sinclair and The Fabulous Five, you won't want to miss out on this awesome opportunity! Be one of the first 100 readers to send in the coupon below and we'll send you a FREE collectible autographed edition of The Fabulous Five Super Edition, MISSING YOU.

This special limited edition will not be available in any bookstore! For a chance to receive this book free, fill in the coupon below (no photocopies or facsimiles allowed), cut it out and send it to:

**FABULOUS FIVE COLLECTOR'S EDITION OFFER
BANTAM BOOKS, YOUNG READERS MARKETING,
DEPT. IGFF
666 FIFTH AVE
New York, NY 10103**

Here's my rush coupon! If I am one of the first 100 readers whose coupon you receive, please send me a FREE specially autographed collectible copy of THE FABULOUS FIVE SUPER EDITION #3: MISSING YOU.

Name: _____ Age:_____

Address: _____

City/State/Prov.:_____

Zip/Postal Code _____

Please allow four to six weeks for delivery. Offer open only to residents of the United States of America, Puerto Rico and Canada. Void where prohibited, taxed or restricted. Bantam Books is not responsible for lost, incomplete or misdirected coupons. If your coupon is not among the first 100 received, we will not be able to send you the special edition. Offer expires June 31, 1991.

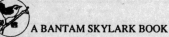 A BANTAM SKYLARK BOOK

Postage paid by Bantam Books
SK43-7/91

Taffy Sinclair is perfectly gorgeous and totally stuck-up. Ask her rival Jana Morgan or anyone else in the sixth grade of Mark Twain Elementary. Once you meet Taffy, life will **never** be the same.

Don't Miss Any of the Terrific Taffy Sinclair Titles from Betsy Haynes!

- ☑ 15819-8 **TAFFY GOES TO HOLLYWOOD** $2.95
- ☐ 15712-4 **THE AGAINST TAFFY SINCLAIR CLUB** $2.75
- ☐ 15693-4 **BLACKMAILED BY TAFFY SINCLAIR** $2.75
- ☐ 15604-7 **TAFFY SINCLAIR AND THE MELANIE MAKEOVER** $2.75
- ☐ 15644-6 **TAFFY SINCLAIR AND THE ROMANCE MACHINE DISASTER** $2.75
- ☐ 15714-0 **TAFFY SINCLAIR AND THE SECRET ADMIRER EPIDEMIC** $2.75
- ☐ 15713-2 **TAFFY SINCLAIR, BABY ASHLEY AND ME** $2.75
- ☐ 15647-0 **TAFFY SINCLAIR, QUEEN OF THE SOAPS** $2.75
- ☐ 15607-1 **THE TRUTH ABOUT TAFFY SINCLAIR** $2.95

Follow the adventures of Jana and the rest of **THE FABULOUS FIVE** in a new series by Betsy Haynes.

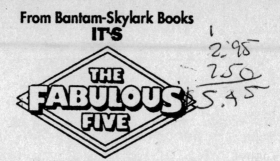